E30

A tale of two murders

A strange man was Stephen Gazeley. Sometimes he could be witty, delightful and amusing, charm personified indeed. But on other occasions, as his homely sister Hilda knew very well, the familiar features would darken into a scowl and he would seem to snarl at those who dared to cross his path.

One such person was his daughter, Katherine, engaged to young Colin Luckett. Her father was obviously against the match. But why did he have such a pronounced aversion to the Luckett family whom he hardly knew? And why couldn't Hilda trust his civil politeness to Colin? What malicious thoughts and plots did it conceal?

When the murder came, it was swift and sudden. The facts that gradually came to light afterwards made Hilda realise how much she had accepted over the years. How could she have been so blind to what was happening around her?

In this baffling tale, Elizabeth Ferrars will once more delight her many readers who have come to expect such a high standard of thrills and excitement from her.

Books by Elizabeth Ferrars

The other devil's name
Unreasonable doubt
I met murder
The crime and the crystal
Root of all evil
Something wicked
Death of a minor character
Skeleton in search of a cupboard
Thinner than water
Experiment with death
Frog in the throat
Designs on life
Witness before the fact
In at the kill
Last will and testament
Murders anonymous
The pretty pink shroud
Blood flies upwards
The cup and the lip
Drowned rat
Alive and dead
Hanged man's house
The small world of murder
Foot in the grave
Breath of suspicion
A stranger and afraid
The seven sleepers
The swaying pillars
No peace for the wicked
I, said the fly
Murder moves in
Murder among friends
Furnished for murder

The busy body
Fear the light
Murder in time
The doubly dead
A legal fiction
Ninth life
Zero at the bone
A tale of two murders
With murder in mind
Alibi for a witch
March hare murders
Hunt the tortoise
The lying voices
Milk of human kindness
The clock that wouldn't stop
Enough to kill a horse
Always say die
The sleeping dogs
Count the cost
Death in botanists bay
Your neck in a noose
Don't monkey with murder
Give a corpse a bad name
Remove the bodies
Skeleton staff
The wandering widows
Come and be killed
Furnished for murder
Trial by fury
Woman slaughter
Smoke without fire
Sleep of the unjust

A TALE OF TWO MURDERS

Elizabeth Ferrars

Constable London

First published 1959
by William Collins Sons & Co Ltd
Copyright © 1959 by M. D. Brown
The right of Elizabeth Ferrars to be
identified as the author of this work
has been asserted by her in accordance
with the Copyright, Designs and
Patents Act 1988
Reprinted 1992
by Constable & Company Ltd
3 The Lanchesters, 162 Fulham Palace Road
London W6 9ER
ISBN 0 09 470860 6
Printed in Great Britain by
St Edmundsbury Press Ltd
Bury St Edmunds, Suffolk

CHAPTER I

It was precisely six forty-five when Mrs. Frearson appeared beside the river. With her head deliberately turned away from the two people who sat on the bench in the garden on the far side of the stream, she walked quickly along the path, in and out among the willows.

"There she goes, our mystery woman," Katherine Gazeley said. "Dead on time. You could set your watch by her."

The woman's dark hair and dark raincoat made her seem little more than a shadow, moving among other shadows.

Hilda Gazeley, Katherine's aunt, seeing the slender figure hurrying past, thought that the light of the fading sunset gave her a look so solitary and sombre that something disturbing crept into the mere act of watching her.

"All the same, you can't really call her a mystery woman, when we know all about her," Hilda said.

"You don't imagine we do know all about her, do you?"

"Not *all* about her, no."

"Not very much about her. Almost nothing about her. Only what we've been told by people who probably don't know much themselves."

"She likes to take a walk in the evening, that's all there really is to know, and she likes to look at the sunset, just as I do," Hilda said.

"Only she never stands still to look at it."

"Perhaps she does when we aren't here."

"Well, there you are. Isn't there something mysterious about caring whether we're here or not?"

"It just happens she likes her own company, I suppose." As the angle of the house behind them cut off

Mrs. Frearson from their view, Hilda Gazeley turned her head and looked into her niece's face. " You said you wanted to talk to me about something in particular."

" Yes."

Hilda thought that she knew what was coming. But that might not help her much to give the right answer.

As she waited for Katherine to go on, the sky, which was tinged with a clear, golden light, was suddenly filled with starlings. They wheeled overhead in a great speckled cloud, straight towards the sunset, then down upon the trees that grew amongst the ruins on the far side of the river.

Though these were too far away for the sound of the birds' chattering to reach the two women in the garden, they could see clearly, against the copper blaze of the west, a great stir among the branches, a coming and going from tree to tree among the ruins of the old nunnery.

This was one of the sights of the evening that Hilda loved, this orderly return to their roost, from whatever direction, of that incalculable number of birds. But Katherine had not lifted her eyes to watch it.

" Why," she said suddenly, in a low tone, " that's what I've got to know—*why* should there be any difficulty about Colin? "

Turning her head, she looked sharply at Hilda.

There was a strong resemblance between the niece and the aunt, though the one was only twenty-two years old and the other twenty years older. Neither was tall, and each in her build had a softness of outline, which in Katherine was supple and delicate, in Hilda was rounded out to plumpness, yet was essentially the same in them both. The face of each was wide across the cheekbones, sloping in to a small, pointed chin. Both had thick, dark brown hair. But in their expressions, in their grey eyes, as they regarded one another, there was no resemblance. Katherine's look was challenging, restless, combative.

Hilda's was uncertain and mild. The smile that had come faintly to her face as she watched the starlings had stayed there, giving her an air of fixed and slightly foolish calm.

"But this is the first you've said about any difficulty," she said. "What kind of difficulty?"

"That I've *said*! I've tried over and over again to talk about it, ever since I first met Colin," Katherine said. "But I've only to mention his name for a thick cloud of silence to come down on the room. Well, why? That's all I'm asking at the moment—why? What have you and Father got against him?"

"I've nothing against him," Hilda said.

"Father, then?"

"Nothing either, I'm sure. If he had . . ."

"Well?"

"Oh, he'd have spoken about it."

"And he hasn't?"

There was only the shortest of pauses before Hilda said, "No."

"Yet have you been acting as people are supposed to act when one gets engaged to be married?"

"But truly I'm all at sea," Hilda said. "I didn't know—I didn't realise you felt——"

"That you and Father are against us?"

"And even if either of us was, at your age . . ."

"Oh, I know you can't stop our getting married. But *why*——?" Katherine's voice went thin. "Why should you want to?"

Blaming herself for not having prepared herself better for this crisis, and because, at the best of times, she always thought so slowly, Hilda hunted for words that would soften the edge of Katherine's suspicion, without being actually untrue.

"I hardly know Colin," she said at last. "I like what I've seen of him. The quarrel, if you can call it a quarrel——"

"Ah, you admit there is one!"

"Well, it's with his parents," Hilda said. "We just don't like the way they've behaved to us. But it isn't anything important."

"Is that what Father will say, that it isn't important?"

"I imagine so."

Katherine laughed. She stood up. She walked a few steps away and stood looking towards the river and to the fields beyond it, with the broken stone walls rising up blackly out of their midst.

The starlings were gradually settling for the night among the branches of the elms. Only a few birds were darting back and forth, still restless and busy in the intricate organisation of their private affairs. Beyond the fields, a single light shone in a window.

Katherine gestured towards the river, a dark strip of water under the drooping willows.

"It's the same as your saying that that woman takes walks to look at the sunset. You don't want to see the facts."

"What facts do you mean?"

"That Mrs. Frearson really *is* a mystery woman—and that Father hates Colin and his family, *hates* them!"

"I don't understand," Hilda said helplessly. "What's the connection between Mrs. Frearson and Colin's family? I don't believe they even know one another."

"There's no connection, that I know of."

"Then why . . .?"

"Because you're the same about them both," Katherine said. "You always pretend there's nothing queer about anything. Nothing wrong."

Hilda did not try to answer this. She sat quietly watching Katherine, with only an added stillness in her small, plump body to show that she had heard.

Katherine turned and faced her. She gazed at her steadily. At first it was with derision in her eyes, but then with a look of abruptly giving in to some gentler feeling in herself, a look which, as Hilda knew, would generally appear in the end, if one could wait for it.

"There, I'm sorry," Katherine said. "I began at the wrong end. I started to quarrel with you before you even knew what I was talking about. If I'd kept my head better, you wouldn't have been so afraid of admitting that there are difficulties about my getting married."

"The difficulties," Hilda said, "the importance of which you're mostly imagining, are simply that Colin's parents don't like us. I don't know why. When I first came here to look after you, they seemed to be good friends of Stephen's, and were very kind to me. But later their attitude changed. They didn't exactly refuse to know us any more, but they became very rude and abrupt, as if they despised us. I didn't like it, so I decided not to see any more of them. But Stephen thought I was foolish. He said it was just their way. He's really much more tolerant of people's peculiarities than I am. Look at the way he puts up with that awful Jim Kent. And I'm sure he has nothing against Colin."

"I suppose you'll always be loyal to Father, whatever he makes you go through," Katherine said. "You'll never admit there's anything wrong about him. But people always turn against him sooner or later, don't they, as—as mother did, before she died? There must be a reason for that."

"I don't know why you always speak as if your mother turned against him," Hilda said. "It simply isn't true. And I think Stephen has as many friends as most people."

The derisive light was back in Katherine's eyes.

"I ought to have known we couldn't discuss things," she said. "But you might tell Father what I've been asking you. And you might tell him too that whatever the trouble is, I'm not going to let it make any difference to Colin and me."

"I can't see why you shouldn't tell him that yourself," Hilda said.

"Oh well..." Katherine shrugged her shoulders.

The gesture implied that she was not to be blamed now for what might happen. She had made her attempt at communication and had failed. With a wry smile on her face, she walked away round the corner of the house, leaving Hilda alone on the bench in the garden.

The bench was against the blank wall at the end of the house, facing southwards towards a small wood, where the brown tinge of autumn was just beginning to show. Narrow lawns, stretching on one side to the river bank, and on the other to a low, stone wall that divided the garden from the road, surrounded the whole long, narrow house. The spot was very quiet and sheltered. Though there were several cottages at the crossroads beyond the wood, there was no other house in sight, except for the one where the single light shone, half a mile away, beyond the ruins, the house where Mrs. Frearson lived.

As the sunset faded, this light shone brighter. At the same time, Hilda's shadow, lying alongside her on the grass, lost its sharp outlines and grew dim in the deepening twilight.

After a few minutes of sitting there alone, thinking uneasily, she stood up, wrapped her knitted jacket closely around her and turned to follow Katherine indoors. As she did so, her shadow leapt ahead of her towards the road, rearing up the garden wall and having its head cut off by the stone coping. Decapitated, the shadow took a couple of steps beside her, then was lost, as the corner of the house blotted out the last of the glow in the western sky.

In spite of what she had said to Katherine about telling her father herself of what worried her in his attitude towards the man she intended to marry, Hilda's intention was to find her brother Stephen immediately and warn him of what was probably coming. For the six years that she had lived with them, she had done her best to act as a bridge between father and daughter, though without ever admitting to either, or even entirely to herself, that such a bridge was necessary. Instinctively, and largely to reduce the strain in her own life, she continually reported to each a softened version of the words and acts of the other, and with the innocence that was a part of her own peace-loving, not very alert mind, assumed that neither doubted her.

Stephen, she thought now, would be in his study. Its french window faced, as most of the windows of this house so annoyingly did, towards the road instead of the river, and now, as she went up the path, was the first that she came to. She would have gone straight to it to find Stephen, if, as she turned towards the glass doors to open them, a movement at the far end of the garden had not caught her eye.

It was Jim Kent, the gardener, at work among the vegetables.

Hilda paused. For some time now, whenever she had seen him, she had felt an intense desire to look the other way, to become engrossed in something else, to pretend that she had not seen him. Yet she seldom let herself yield to the desire. To have done so would have seemed abject and rather ridiculous. So, with a sharp sigh, she walked on past Stephen's window and on across the grass, which was moist with a heavy dew, until she stood a few feet away from the man, whose broad back was towards her as he forked over the ground where the peas had stood in the summer.

" You're working very late, Jim," she said. " Isn't it time you went home? "

He neither stopped working, nor looked round at her.

" Do it now, save doing it next week," he said in a surly tone.

" But you're always putting in extra time."

" Whose business is that but mine? "

" Well, doesn't your wife want you at home sometimes? "

He straightened up then and regarded her. He was a big man, solid and quiet-looking, about forty years old. His light blue eyes had a glazed, withdrawn look.

"What my wife wants or doesn't want isn't your business, that I know of," he said.

Hilda's cheeks burnt. She started to answer, then snapped her lips shut, turned and walked away.

Going to the window of Stephen's study, opening it and stepping into the room, she spoke at once, hurriedly, distractedly, not of Katherine and Colin, but of Jim Kent, the gardener.

"He's been rude again, Stephen—quite horribly rude, when I was only meaning to be pleasant to him. You've got to get rid of him. I can't stand having anyone like that around. I think perhaps he's a bit mad. He frightens me."

Stephen Gazeley lowered the evening paper that he had been reading.

"Don't be too hard on him," he said. "He's a wonderful worker, and I dare say he's got his troubles."

Stephen was a short man, no taller than Hilda, but wide in the shoulders and a little portly, so that he comfortably filled the big, square-armed chair. The family resemblance between him and his sister showed as plainly as that between her and Katherine. He had the width across the cheekbones, the pointed chin and grey eyes. But his cheeks were fuller and pinker than Hilda's, and the flesh was thicker under the chin, while his hair, which had once been the same brown as hers, was almost white. He wore gold-rimmed spectacles, behind which his eyes had a look of cool good nature. He was ten years the older.

"Sit down," he said. "Make yourself comfortable. And don't worry about Jim."

"I can't help worrying."

Hilda looked round for a chair, but was too distraught to make up her mind where to sit. This room, with its big desk, filing cabinets and shelves of sombre-looking legal books, had always seemed to her very positively a place where she did not belong, and she seldom stayed in it for long enough to make sitting down worth while.

" I worry every time he speaks to me like that," she said, " as if he detested me. I'd sooner dig every inch of the garden myself than have a man around who loathes me so."

" I'm sure he doesn't loathe you," Stpehen said. " He's a bit gruff, that's all. And as I said, I think he has troubles at home."

He thrust a packet of cigarettes towards her. She took one and lit it with a not very steady hand.

" And why does he stay on and on, instead of just doing his four hours? " she asked. " You don't pay him extra, do you? "

" Oh no."

" Well, it isn't natural."

" Probably he's glad of a reason for staying away from home," Stephen said. " And he may even like to work."

" For people he seems to hate as he hates us? "

" I haven't seen any signs of his hating me. We did have a bit of a row once, but he soon got over it. Of course, I don't interfere with him. For the most part, I let him instruct me in what needs doing in the garden."

" I don't interfere with him either," Hilda said, " but just occasionally I try to say something friendly. When he first came, he didn't seem to mind that. He used to talk about the garden. He used to tell me about the children. He seemed very proud of them. He wanted to talk about them. But if I ask him about them now, he almost shows his teeth at me."

" The children aren't his, you know."

" Aren't . . . ? Oh, you mean they're adopted. Yes, but both he and his wife wanted them, because of their having none of their own. He told me so himself."

" It may not have worked out as they hoped. And the

children aren't actually adopted. They're foster-children from that church-home in Ledslowe. That means they came from bad homes originally, and may be turning out badly themselves. Or the authorities may be dissatisfied with the way they're being looked after. They can sometimes be very unreasonable about that sort of thing."

Hilda took a couple of quick pulls at her cigarette. She did not smoke often, and now let the smoke get in her eyes. Rubbing them with the back of her hand, she said, " It wasn't Jim Kent I came in here to talk about."

" No," Stephen said, " it was Katherine, wasn't it? "

She arched her eyebrows at him, worried that he should know this already.

He smiled and explained, " I saw her go past the window with a certain sardonic look on her face, which I know generally means trouble. What is it? "

Hilda turned away from him and looked out of the window. There was not much to be seen there, a strip of grass, a length of garden wall, with a patch illuminated, against the deepening twilight, by the light in the room, and beyond the wall a row of shaggy pines, standing out darkly against the greenish sky.

" You won't like it," she said.

" Something to do with her affair with young Luckett? What did you say to her? "

" I told her to talk to you herself."

" Advice she hasn't taken."

" She will presently."

" Will she? She's past the age when I feel I can affect the situation much. She knows that."

" Yes, but she's very worried."

" Serves her right."

He said it quietly, without animosity, yet Hilda glanced at him quickly.

" She wanted to know what we had against Colin," she said. " I told her, nothing."

"Quite right," Stephen said. "We haven't."

"Or his family either—anything serious, I mean."

"Except that none of them is really any good. Too much money and too little in the way of manners. But that's her look out, not ours. Apart from that . . ."

"Well?"

"They're no good," he said in a louder tone.

There was a glint in his eyes, a flash that momentarily shattered their impersonal good nature.

"You were going to say something else as well," Hilda said.

"There's not much else to say, is there?"

"I think the main thing that's the matter with them," she said, "is just that they don't like us. They used to at first, then they changed their minds—almost, you know, as Jim Kent seems to have changed his mind."

"Oh, come," Stephen said. "That's rather different, isn't it? If Jim didn't like us, he wouldn't work for us. He's a good fellow, Hilda, he really is. He's just a bit rough and moody."

"He wasn't rough and moody when he first started working here. And as Katherine said——" She stopped. She puffed at her cigarette and coughed.

She had very nearly told Stephen what Katherine had said about people always sooner or later turning against him. And it wasn't true. It wasn't in the least true. He had plenty of friends, far more than she had herself, and some of them very old friends, like Nelson Wingard, who was coming to visit them next week-end.

"I ought to go and get the supper," she said.

Stephen's upper lip lifted high off his teeth in a faintly mocking smile.

"It isn't often safe to quote Katherine to me, is it? Poor Hilda, we work you hard between us."

"It would be easier for me if only I understood why you don't get on better," she said.

"There's nothing to understand. Katherine doesn't trust me, that's all. And that's my own fault—I know it. And in this instance, she knows I don't like the Lucketts, but thinks you might be persuaded into liking them. You're very easily persuaded into liking people—except our poor gardener."

"Our poor gardener's the only person I've ever known who made me feel he hated me," she said. "It frightens me."

Stephen gave an amused shake of his head. The smile was still on his face, a smile that showed so much of his upper teeth that, not for the first time, Hilda thought that someone who did not know him well might mistake it for a snarl.

"You shouldn't let people frighten you," Stephen said. "They really aren't worth it."

CHAPTER II

ON THE NEXT Friday evening, when Stephen's old friend, Nelson Wingard, arrived from London, there was no brilliant sunset, but only a dim, violet tinge along a misty horizon. It made the home-coming starlings seem like small, stirring specks of the coming darkness.

Sitting beside Hilda on the garden bench, Nelson watched the sight with concentration. One of the reasons for his frequent visits to the Gazeleys was to paint the birds that were to be seen along the river banks. A solicitor, like Stephen, Nelson was a bachelor who lived in a service-flat in Knightsbridge, performing his work, so he said himself, with bare, uninterested adequacy, while waiting, week by week, for the day when he could escape from it to his birds and his painting.

He was a tall man, spare, round-shouldered, bald, and, but for the tan on his long, thin face and something nervously observant in his glance, would have looked merely a prim, sedentary, professional man, going to seed too soon for his forty-nine years.

With his gaze on the starlings, settling down among the trees, he said, " And when Katherine marries and goes away, what are you going to do, Hilda? Stay here with Stephen? "

" Of course."

" Why? "

" Why——? " She returned his look with surprise. Then she had the feeling that her cheeks were reddening. For once or twice during the last few days, the thought had come to her mind—no more than the thought, no more than a faintly coloured, passing daydream—that when Katherine married, she might just possibly go away, go back to London, to her old job in the library, have an income of her own again, and a home that was all her own.

" That would be a nice way to treat him, certainly, walking out on him just when he's lost Katherine," she said, " and when he's looked after me all this time."

" Not for nothing," Nelson said precisely. " The obligation, if any, is on his side. But the question is, do you really want to stay with him? "

" Why shouldn't I? "

" That isn't an answer. Do you, or don't you? " There was pedantic insistence in his voice, a determination to drag an answer out of her.

If Hilda had not known Nelson as well as she did, she might have mistaken the reason for this interest in her feelings. Once, about four years ago, when he had been showing it rather more officiously than usual, she had made a very considerable mistake about it. She had thought that he was falling in love with her. Now this error seemed funny. The very idea of Nelson falling in love with anyone seemed funny. But at the time, although her own feelings had not really been much roused, the suddenness with which he had sheered away from her, rushing off for safety to his flat in Knightsbridge, and not coming for another visit for over a year, had not seemed amusing. It had been embarrassing and humiliating.

Yet there had been a certain compensation for the minor pain of the incident. Stephen, apparently guessing, and perhaps exaggerating the strength of her feelings for Nelson, and wanting to comfort her, had suddenly made her a present of a beautiful coat of Persian lamb. Normally a careful man, who spent his money with a certain reluctance, such gifts from him were rare. Remodelled since that time, the coat was still one of Hilda's most prized possessions.

"You're an old busybody, Nelson," she said equably. "That's what's the matter with you. What does it matter to you if I go or stay?"

"So you'll stay, you'll give up the rest of your life to him," he said, as if he resented this arrangement.

"Can you suggest anything better I could do with it?"

"Can't you think of something yourself? Aren't you bored here? Aren't you lonely? You used to be a bright sort of girl, Hilda. When you first came here you'd lots of friends and lots of interests. Of course I know someone had to help with Katherine when Amabel died, but the girl's been grown up for some time and now she's actually getting married and going away. By the way, how soon is she getting married?"

"Not for some time, I imagine. Colin's still at Oxford."

"That needn't stop them," Nelson said.

"Don't you think perhaps they should wait till he's got a job?"

"No. If they want to marry, tell them to get on with it."

"And what will they live on?"

"What are they living on now? He's living on his family, I suppose, and Katherine's got a job, hasn't she? Why shouldn't that arrangement continue?"

"But I'm not at all sure that would be a good thing," Hilda said.

"Why not? Would Stephen object? Would he try to stop them marrying if the boy hadn't a job?"

"I don't know. We haven't even discussed it."

"Would Colin's family object?"

"I don't know. Perhaps. I really don't know. I haven't seen any of them for a long time."

"What, not even Colin himself?"

"Well, as a matter of fact, no."

"Ah," Nelson said with satisfaction, the satisfaction of having been right about something. "So there *has* been trouble about this engagement. I thought there must have been. And that's why I'm telling you, my dear, if they really want to get married, see that they get on with it quickly. Give Stephen time and he'll manage things so that the marriage never happens at all."

"But there hasn't been any trouble, Nelson—certainly not from Stephen."

He gave her a tight-lipped smile. "No? Then it's only because he thinks there's no hurry. He's a jealous devil, Hilda. You ought to know that."

"Jealous? Oh, you mean that he'll miss Katherine and won't like it when she leaves us? Well, I'll miss her too, but I know it's got to happen some time."

"Stephen isn't very good at accepting the fact that anything has to happen if he doesn't want it to."

She gave an uneasy laugh. It was not unusual for Nelson to say that sort of thing, and she accepted it generally as a by-product of his affection for Stephen, an affection proved by his frequent visits and by all the long evenings that he and Stephen spent amicably together over chess and a bottle of whisky. All the same, it seemed to her a spiteful way to talk, and she had never much liked it.

"If anyone tries to interfere with this marriage, Nelson, it won't be Stephen or me, it'll be the Lucketts," she said. "But even if they aren't particularly pleased about it, I don't believe they'll go so far as trying to interfere. Valerie Luckett might like to. She's a difficult person. She's spoiled and arrogant. You never know where you are with her. But her husband's a quiet sort of man, very wrapped up in his farm, and I don't think there's any reason to fear——"

She stopped. From behind the bushes on the far side of the river, a slight figure had just emerged and was walking rapidly along the path, disappearing and reappearing among the clumps of willow.

"There she goes, our local mystery," Hilda said.

Nelson frowned at the interruption. But as he watched the dark-clad, hurrying figure, his eyes grew interested.

"Odd-looking woman," he remarked.

"When you see her close to, she's quite beautiful," Hilda said.

"Who is she?"

"She's a Mrs. Frearson. She lives over there, in that house where you can see the light. She and her sister, Miss Perriman, have taken it furnished for a year. They came about three months ago. I called and found the sister quite friendly. But Mrs. Frearson won't meet anyone at all. And every day, always at just this time, she takes this walk, and as she passes here, she looks away, as if she's afraid we might say good evening and she'd have to answer."

"What d'you suppose is the matter with her?" Nelson asked.

"I don't know."

He withdrew his gaze from the strange woman, hastening along on her lonely walk, and turned again to Hilda. But then his eyes, which always seemed to Hilda more observant, more penetrating than looked right in his long, lawyer's face, suddenly went back to Mrs. Frearson and he watched her without speaking until she was out of sight.

Hilda took the chance to say, " Now, if I don't get on with the supper, you and Stephen won't have much time for your game of chess."

As she stood up, he looked at her, frowning again, as if he meant to go back to the subject of Stephen. Yet all that he said was, " All right, and I expect that means there's time for me to go along to the Bunch of Flowers for a quick one, doesn't it? "

She agreed, though with an uncomfortable feeling that in his present mood, Nelson would probably make it a quick half-dozen.

If he did, there was no sign of it at supper. Yet later that evening he and Stephen had a quarrel.

It was not the first that they had had during the years of their long friendship, and when Hilda, lying in bed, heard their raised voices from downstairs, she reminded herself that there was no need to worry about it. It was irritating, because it kept her awake, and shouting like that over a game of chess was a childish way for two middle-aged men to behave, but still there was no need to worry about it. They would probably have forgotten all about it in the morning.

But next morning, after an early and silent breakfast, Stephen took the car and went to his office in Ledslowe, the small market town five miles off. Nelson had his breakfast much later, then took his paints and his easel and settled down for a day's painting on the far side of the river. He came in for lunch, but did not talk or linger over it, and so, since Katherine, who was assistant matron in a girls' school in the neighbourhood, but was free on Saturdays, had disappeared early without saying where she was going, Hilda had most of the day to herself. Then, at six o'clock, when she was setting out glasses and a decanter of sherry in the living-room, Katherine suddenly appeared at her elbow with Colin Luckett beside her.

It took Hilda by surprise and for a moment she showed it.

Colin, smiling, said laconically, " I told Katherine I ought not to have come like this, without any invitation."

But he did not look as if his self-assurance was much disturbed by the thought. He had, as usual, the calm air of taking himself and others for granted that astonished Hilda whenever she met him. She wondered how anyone of Colin's age had had the chance to acquire such poise.

Yet his self-confidence was not aggressive. It was quiet and good-mannered. And probably, Hilda thought, she would have been less inclined to a slight distrust of him if his good looks had not reminded her so strongly of his mother.

He had her very blue eyes and oval face, her coppery hair and subtly shaped mouth. Like her, he was slight in build, of medium height and neat and quick in his movements. Of his father, a big, dark, heavy man, there was almost no trace in him.

Recovering herself, Hilda held out a hand to him.

" Katherine's only mistake was not to bring you sooner," she said.

" I told her that too, but she chose her own time." He turned to Katherine. " And I do whatever she wants—don't I, Katherine? "

A pink flush came into Katherine's cheeks and her grey eyes grew starry. It was one of her moments of beauty. Something intimate in her, something normally secret, flashed out in her face and touched its young prettiness with a glow so vivid that Hilda found herself having to turn aside and start fumbling with the decanter of sherry.

" You must make her happy," she said. " If you don't, we shall never forgive you."

" I shall never forgive myself either."

"That's all we care about, my brother and I. We love her very much ourselves, you see."

"Then we must talk more about that some time," Colin said. "I like to talk about her. I talk about her nearly all the time, to her face or behind her back, to myself or to anyone who'll listen."

"Yes, we can talk some time," Hilda said. "But now—now I'll go and fetch my brother and we'll drink to your happiness together."

"Hilda——" Katherine began. Then, as Hilda, in turning to the door, paused to listen to her, she shook her head. "No," she said, "go on. Just tell him Colin's here."

She slid an arm through Colin's, standing close to him.

Hilda went to Stephen's study. She found him sitting in his usual chair, in a position of curious rigidity. He was staring blindly at the window.

"I know, I know," he said without turning his head. "I saw them come. I saw them come in triumph."

"Well, they do look happy," Hilda said.

"Happy!" he said sharply. "That isn't what I said. I said in triumph. The triumph of youth over age, of the future over the past. It's death I saw walking past that window."

"Stephen!"

"Well, face it, face it! To those two now you and I might as well be dead. Our usefulness is over."

"Even if that were so . . ."

"Ah, I know what's coming now. Even if that were so, we should accept it gracefully, generously. And isn't that what I've done?"

"Yes, on the whole you've seemed to take it very well," she said.

"I hope I know how to make the appropriate gestures."

"Considering, I mean, our relations with the Lucketts."

"The Lucketts—I can deal with the Lucketts! But my own child, Katherine, how am I to deal with her?"

"Do you mean . . .?" She paused uneasily.

It was very unfortunate, he was in an abominable mood. It must somehow have been Nelson's fault, she thought, the result of that quarrel last night. Nelson had been putting his foot in it, saying the sort of thing to Stephen that he had said to her, and naturally upsetting him.

"You don't mean, do you, that you're thinking of interfering with this marriage?" she said.

"Is that what I said?" Stephen asked.

"I'm not sure."

His little laugh had an edge on it.

"It's so pleasant to talk to you, Hilda. You have a capacity, which I admire as much as I admire any other remarkable intellectual attainment, for deliberately not understanding anything you'd sooner not understand."

"Then that *is* what you meant."

"How do you suppose I *could* interfere with this marriage, even if I'd like to?"

"I don't know."

"Then why ask the question?"

"Because, when I see a certain look on your face——"

"Well?"

"Oh, it doesn't matter. You're just in one of your horrid moods. But do try not to upset Katherine."

"I've never discovered what upsets Katherine and what doesn't."

"Well, just be nice to her. Don't—don't grudge her her happiness."

He bounced up out of his chair.

"It's my impression, you know, that I've never grudged that child anything."

"Then don't start now."

He stared at her hard for a moment, a short, portly man, rather redder in the face than usual, with his upper lip lifting off his teeth in his snarling smile. Then suddenly he started to laugh. He jerked down his waistcoat, patted his stomach, laughed again and set off to the living-room.

Hilda followed him anxiously. She knew how swiftly his moods could change, particularly if it was a question of making a favourable impression on some relative stranger, but just then it would have seemed to her too much to hope that, between one sentence and the next, the bitter, menacing tone in which he had been speaking to her could alter to one of the friendliest charm.

Yet that was what happened.

One of Stephen's hands fell on Katherine's shoulder. The other hand went out to Colin, to grasp one of his and shake it warmly.

"You know, it isn't my fault," Stephen said, looking into the young man's face, "that we don't already know each other much better than we do. We must put that right, eh?"

"I hope we can," Colin answered, rather coolly, all considered.

"And you, my dear..." Stephen looked into his daughter's face. He seemed about to say more to her, then cleared his throat loudly, started to pat her shoulder in a fumbling gesture of tenderness and turned again to Colin.

"You'll stay to dinner, won't you? Hilda, I shan't be upsetting all the housekeeping arrangements, shall I, if I ask this young man to stay to dinner?"

With emotion, Hilda answered, "Not if he can eat stew."

"Thank you," Colin said. "It's very good of you, but I——" He paused. Something seemed to pass between him and Katherine. He looked down. "Thank you, I should like to."

As if something had just occurred which she had believed wholly impossible, Katherine exclaimed unintelligibly, and, quite uncharacteristically, flung her arms round her father's neck.

Stephen stroked her hair. He cleared his throat again.
"You see, you see," he said, "you should have trusted me, you shouldn't have worried, should you?" His hoarse voice faded. Over Katherine's head, his eyes met Hilda's.

With a sense of shock, because for those few moments she had been filled with joy, she saw that there was no feeling of any kind in his eyes. They were as blank as pebbles.

She knew that look. It had always chilled her and scared her. It reminded her that there were certain qualities in her brother that she had never been able to understand. For all her affection for him, it was a look that she could not bear.

"Stephen," she said hurriedly, "the sherry—please pour out the sherry, and we'll all——"

She stopped, because just then she heard footsteps outside the door. As she hesitated, Nelson Wingard came into the room.

He took in the scene before him, smiled genially and asked to be introduced to Colin. Then, as if he were host, he poured out the sherry, and handed round the glasses. The tension went out of the room. Standing on the hearthrug with his back to the empty fireplace, Nelson made ordinary conversation. Or very nearly ordinary conversation. Listening to him, Hilda could not make out whether the feeling she had that it was really not quite ordinary, but had behind it some curious intention, came in fact from the way that Nelson was talking, or was merely the result of her own intention not to meet Stephen's eyes again just yet. So long as he was actually behaving kindly to the two young people, she wanted to be able to forget that look.

"I'm afraid I've just done an extraordinarily stupid thing," Nelson said. He smiled broadly as he said it, relishing something about his own stupidity, and taking pride in it rather than regretting it. "I was taken by surprise, that was the trouble. I was sitting there, just thinking that with the light changing as it was, it was about time to come indoors, but not really wanting to move—enjoying it all too much, you know—the quiet, and the colours in the sky and their reflections in the water—when this woman suddenly appeared at my elbow, and for some cock-eyed reason, I thought I knew her and started to speak to her. And she just took one look at me and streaked for safety!"

He gave a shout of laughter.

"Yes, she took one look at me, thought the worst and ran," he said. "It gave me almost as much of a shock as I'd given her. It seems to me it's years since any sensible woman would have reacted like that to me."

"But you're talking about our mystery woman," Katherine said. "Mrs. Frearson. And, of course, she isn't sensible."

"Thank you, my dear," Nelson said. "That's very simply put. You allay my fears."

"Oh, I didn't mean that," Katherine said. "I only meant——"

"I know, I know." He was still smiling broadly. "But you're perfectly right, the poor thing can't be quite normal. That's why I said I'd done a very stupid thing. By thinking for a moment I knew her, and speaking to her as if I did, I evidently gave her a very bad fright. That's a shame. I'm extremely sorry about it."

Stephen had sat down in an easy-chair. He sipped some sherry.

"I wonder," he said, "why you thought you knew her."

"Perhaps you do," Katherine said. "Perhaps you've seen her before."

Nelson shook his head. "No, I'm sure I haven't. If I had, I shouldn't have forgotten her. Strange as she is, she's very beautiful, very striking. All the same, there's something about her that still seems familiar, as if perhaps I'd seen her photograph some time. Now could that be it?" His eyebrows shot up in astonishment at some thought that he had had. "No," he said. "Of course that's impossible. The woman's dead. All the same, there *is* a resemblance.... That must be why I had the feeling of recognising her. A resemblance. When I think about it, a quite striking resemblance. But I'm very sorry indeed that I upset her. Hilda, if the occasion arises, perhaps you could explain and apologise for me."

"But you haven't told us whom she resembles," Hilda said.

He shook his head again. "I told you, the person I suddenly thought of is dead. Let's not raise her ghost. We've other pleasanter things to think about at the moment."

He raised his glass, smiling across it at Katherine and Colin.

CHAPTER III

THE WEEK-END following Nelson's visit, Stephen went to London.

It was not often that he did this. He was a man who liked to sleep in his own bed, sit in his own arm-chair and eat the food to which he was accustomed. Change made him irritable and gave him headaches, and it was only important matters of business, into which Hilda never inquired, that made him face it.

There were advantages to Hilda in his occasional absences. Among them there was the possibility of accepting certain invitations that he would probably have managed to make her refuse, such as the one that came to the two of them to have tea with Miss Perriman, the sister of the mysterious Mrs. Frearson, on Saturday afternoon. Not that Stephen had shown any dislike of Miss Perriman, but he had a knack of finding irrefutable reasons for refusing most invitations, preferring to be visited in his own home to venturing into one belonging to anyone else. Hilda, on the other hand, was usually glad to get away from the house where she spent all too much of her time.

She had called on Miss Perriman soon after her arrival. The call had been returned, and since then they had met one another a number of times about the village. Unlike Mrs. Frearson, Miss Perriman seemed to be friendly, and ready to take a moderate interest in village life. Except that she too was tall, only the faintest of resemblances marked her relationship to her sister. This, seen most clearly at a first glance, grew progressively harder to perceive as the totally dissimilar personalities of the two women revealed themselves.

Miss Perriman was big and thick-set, with a square, weather-beaten face and with grey hair, cut in a straight bob. She was about fifty, which was and at least fifteen years older than her sister. But there was so much vigorous life in her that it was easy to imagine her outliving the younger, frail-looking woman into a vital, independent old age.

Her youth was in some ways harder to imagine, though in appearance, perhaps, she had not changed much. The bobbed hair, the too-short skirt, the heavy shoes, might have been the uniform of her schooldays, clung to in frightened defiance of her own femininity. Yet there was a certain reckless gleam in her eye which did not altogether fit with the kind of life that she was leading now.

The house that she and her sister had rented was a small, neat, modern house, set down in the midst of flat fields, with no building near it but the remains of the old nunnery. Hilda had tea alone with Miss Perriman in the small, bright sitting-room, from the window of which she could see her own home. Whether Mrs. Frearson was out, or merely in hiding from the visitor, was left unexplained, yet almost at once, almost as soon as the tea had been poured out and the toasted tea-cakes handed, Miss Perriman began to talk about her.

She told Hilda that her sister had recently lost her husband in a car-accident in which Mrs. Frearson herself had been injured, that because of her emotional state her recovery had been very slow, and that though now she was physically well, she was still far from being the person that she had once been.

" But she's been getting on much better since we came here," Miss Perriman said, when Hilda had expressed her sympathy. " She likes the quiet. I can't really get used to that, because she used not to be the sort of person who liked a quiet life at all. She'd never live anywhere but London, and she loved parties and having people around her. Loved them a bit too much, I used to think. But then parties have never been much in my line, so I can't really say. To someone like her, someone so beautiful, I mean, I suppose it's natural to be constantly surrounded by people." She crossed one long leg over the other, her short skirt slipping up above her knees. " She *is* a beauty, shouldn't you say? "

" Oh, she is," Hilda said. " She's quite remarkable."

" Remarkable," Miss Perriman said quickly. " Yes, that's the word. You mean she's a person you'd notice, a person you'd remember."

" Yes, I think so, though as for remembering," Hilda said, wondering why the other woman was watching her so intently, " I'm afraid I've no memory at all for names and faces."

" Ah, that's middle-age, my dear," Miss Perriman said with a laugh. " I've the same failing. That's to say, I'm not bad at faces in themselves, but my difficulty is to fix the right names to them. For instance, the other day . . ." She took a bite of tea-cake. Her voice came muffled by the doughy mouthful. " The other day I was out for a walk, and I came on a man painting by the river, opposite your house, and for a moment I was absolutely sure that we'd met before, that his name was Robinson and that I'd met him on a cruise in the Ægean. Yet later on, when I got home, I remembered quite clearly that Mr. Robinson had been short and bald and that he came from Lancashire. So what's puzzling me now is who the man painting can really have been."

" Oh, that must have been Mr. Wingard, a friend who was staying with us," Hilda said.

" Wingard? " Miss Perriman said. " Who is he? Where does he live? "

" He lives in London. He's a solicitor. But the real passion of his life is painting birds," Hilda said. " He comes here quite often."

" No, I don't know him, I'm sure I don't," Miss Perriman said. " I suppose he just reminded me of someone I've seen some time." The sentence ended on a questioning note, as if she expected Hilda to confirm or contradict this.

" The curious thing is, that's just what he said about your sister," Hilda said. " But he didn't mention that he'd seen you as well."

" That doesn't surprise me," Miss Perriman said with a wry smile. " It happens to me all the time. Once people have seen Leslie, they have a way of forgetting that they've seen me too."

" Well, I should think you must all have met somewhere," Hilda said. " Next time he comes, you must come to see us, then you can talk it over."

" Yes, that would be very nice," Miss Perriman said uncertainly, as if she were not really sure that it would be nice at all, and her glance strayed away from Hilda's face, rested for a moment on a bowl of roses, then on a parchment-shaded lamp, then on some books, then on a gilt-framed mirror, until, meeting her own eyes in the mirror, she gave a sharp shudder.

For a moment she looked as if she had just discovered that the cheerful little room, with its chintz-covered chairs, pale, painted walls and ruffled curtains, were some fearful trap, into which she had fallen headlong.

Hilda felt sorry for her, she was not sure why. Yet, walking home presently, she felt that there had really been something rather unpleasant about the oblique way in which Miss Perriman had approached the subject of Nelson's encounter with her sister. For that surely was what she had been doing. And why should it matter whether or not Nelson had recognised her? Was Mrs. Frearson a film star, or royalty incognito, or a wanted criminal, that it could matter?

Thinking of these things, Hilda walked home along the quiet road taken by Mrs. Frearson every evening. It led to a bridge across the river, then on to crossroads, where it met at right-angles the road that passed the Gazeleys' house.

Mrs. Frearson never went as far as the bridge. She always turned off the road just before she reached it, going through a turnstile and down on to the path along the river bank. This led her to where another road crossed the river, and she took this road back to her home.

It was a nice enough walk, Hilda thought, as she reached the gate and paused there, looking down at the river. But it was not the only nice walk in the neighbourhood, and never to vary it argued a very curious turn of mind, as curious, in its way, as a turn of mind that led one to caring whether or not one had been seen before by Nelson Wingard.

Hilda went on over the bridge, and just beyond it came face to face with Jim Kent and his family.

They lived in one of the cottages at the crossroads, and they were out now for a stroll together. Maureen Kent, a slight, dark-haired young woman, with a thin, animated face and a great deal of restless energy, which had been a trouble to her before she had had the children to care for, had her arm linked through her husband's. The two children, both girls, aged about six and five, were busy, a little way ahead of their foster parents, with a small, battered tricycle. Jim Kent, keeping a protective eye on them, was smiling as he made some remark to his wife.

The smile endured on his face, like something that he had forgotten about, for a moment after he had seen Hilda, but the meaning had drained out of it.

Yet his wife called out cheerfully, "Good evening, Miss Gazeley. It's a nice evening, isn't it? We're just taking the girls for a little walk before I give them their tea. How d'you think they're looking, Miss Gazeley? Not like when I got them from the home, are they? Haven't they grown? Theresa, Carolyn, say good evening to Miss Gazeley."

Looking at the children, knowing that to satisfy Maureen Kent she must stay and talk about them for a little, though wanting, because of the man who was standing there with his blank, cold face half-turned away from them all and his big hands hanging clenched at his sides, to get away as fast as she could, Hilda said hurriedly, "Yes, they've come on quite amazingly. You've really done wonders for them."

"And they've done wonders for me, Miss Gazeley," Maureen said. "That's the truth. And for Jim too. I can't even remember what it was like without them. They're good girls. I feel about them now like they're my own, and so does Jim. We couldn't think more of them both than we do."

Like a piece of machinery going stiffly into gear, Jim muttered, "That's right." But he kept his gaze several inches to one side of Hilda's face as he said it.

Hilda knew that he had spoken only to prevent his

wife realising the hostility to Hilda that burnt in him so incomprehensibly, and which, it seemed clear, his wife did not share.

Because of this meeting with the Kents, Hilda reached home in a mood of nervous depression, and so went to sit by herself on the bench in the garden and wait for the starlings to fly home into the sunset. Though a light in an upstairs window told her that Katherine was at home, just then Hilda did not want her company.

She sat there brooding on how peaceful it had been in the old days, how free from problems, to arrive back at her own small flat, after her day's work at the library. Not that she had appreciated it at the time. She had taken a long while to get over the shock of the death at Arnhem of the only man with whom she had ever been deeply in love, and life had seemed empty and often desolate. But at least she had had no feeling of being surrounded by mysterious dislike. Naturally quarrels had occurred in the library, but she had known more or less what had caused them, and had not been too inept at making peace.

She was still sitting there, thinking and watching the brightening of the colours in the western sky, when Stephen appeared round the corner of the house.

She looked at him in surprise.

"When did you get back? I thought you weren't coming till to-morrow," she said.

"I got through my business faster than I expected, and came down on the four forty-five."

He sat down beside her, put an arm round her and kissed her on the cheek. It was a gesture that was fairly rare with him.

"Did you have a good day?" she asked.

"Yes, quite good, but it's good to be back. It always is."

Settling himself comfortably on the bench, he looked around him at the river and the garden and the wood with its early tinge of autumn, as if to be able to come back to these things was all the pleasure that he asked in life.

" Still, tell me about London," she said.

" There's really nothing to tell—except that I had lunch with Nelson." He lit a cigarette. " I've just seen Katherine. What d'you think she wants now? She wants me to call on the Lucketts, or invite them here, or something."

" And you said you wouldn't? "

" On the contrary, I said I was perfectly willing to do so. At which she burst into tears and rushed off to her room. My God, what a girl! "

" Well, she's difficult sometimes."

" I suppose she knew all along that they won't respond, but in her daughterly fashion, wants to fix all the blame on me. And I let her down by saying I'd do anything she wanted me to."

Hilda gave a shake of her head. " There was more to it than that, wasn't there? "

" Well, I did begin by saying that I didn't see the point of what she wanted. I reminded her that the Lucketts don't seem to have much use for us. And in that I include their son. I know he doesn't like me, though I've been as pleasant to him as I could manage. That's true—I have, haven't I? "

" Yes," she said.

And so it was. During the past week, Stephen had not only been courteous to Colin, he had also made a surprising effort to efface himself, to withdraw his claims to Katherine's attention, whenever Colin was there. If there had been any discomfort in the atmosphere, it was Colin who had caused it.

He had done this, not by avoiding Stephen any longer, but rather by seeking him out, doing all that he could to set him talking, then himself sitting back to listen with a cool, guarded air into which Hilda had read some deep suspicion of Stephen.

"But I also said," he went on, "what does it matter whether he does or doesn't like me? It's her he's marrying. For some reason she took exception to that point of view."

"It's a little cold-blooded," Hilda said. "I wish we could somehow make peace with the Lucketts. If only we knew for certain what they've got against us.... You see, if Katherine really blew up at you for the reason you said, it must mean she's feeling a great strain in the situation, and that seems so sad, when she ought just to be happy."

"Happy?" Stephen said. "Who's happy? Who's ever happy? If she weren't feeling this strain, she'd be feeling some other. It's her nature, no doubt inherited from me. And as far as I'm concerned, we *are* at peace with the Lucketts. I'll admit I'd be glad if she'd decided to marry into a family with whom relations were a little easier, and there are times when the sight of that arrogant boy, looking at me as if I were something too low to be in the same room with, is almost more than I can bear. But I'm controlling my feelings about him very carefully, and behaving very well." His hand suddenly clutched Hilda's. "Look!" he exclaimed. "Look, there she goes!"

As he spoke, Mrs. Frearson appeared from behind the willows on the far bank of the river, and walked quickly along the path.

After one glance at her, Hilda turned her head to look at Stephen. The tone in which he had spoken had sounded to her so strange, so full of excitement, that for a moment she doubted that he could actually be talking about Mrs. Frearson. But as the strange woman went by, with her long, slightly jerky, yet somehow graceful strides, like the strides of an immature but lovely girl, Stephen sat gazing at her with eyes into which there had come a look of intense interest, while his short, plump body, so at ease a moment before on the garden bench, had suddenly crouched forward.

"Stephen!" Hilda said.

Until Mrs. Frearson had passed out of sight, he took no notice. Then he gave a high-pitched laugh.

"Our mystery woman," he said. "How did you enjoy your tea with her?"

"I didn't see her," Hilda said. "I had tea with Miss Perriman."

"And?"

"And——? What do you mean? It was just Miss Perriman."

"And what did she tell you? That's what I meant. About her sister. Isn't that what she asked you to tea for—to tell you what she wanted you to know about her sister?"

As Hilda looked at him confusedly, he began to laugh again, then he stood up suddenly, and as if he had just remembered some business to which he must attend immediately, disappeared swiftly round the corner of the house.

CHAPTER IV

IT WAS A WEEK later that Hilda met Arthur Luckett.

She was not prepared for it. She was on her way to church, to the evening service. She often went to the evening service in preference to the morning, particularly if Nelson was on one of his visits, as he was again that week-end, since she felt that she owed it to him, as a guest, to provide him, at one o'clock, with roast beef and apple tart. She supposed Katherine must have told the Lucketts of this, for Arthur Luckett was waiting at the churchyard gate, and there was no question that he was waiting there deliberately.

"Good evening, Hilda," he said as they met. "I want very much to talk to you. Can you spare me a little time after the service?"

It surprised her that he called her Hilda. True, they had been on Christian name terms in the old days, the long-ago days of their short friendship, but it felt strange to hear him use the word now.

The black eyes in his heavy, tanned face watched her intently. He was a big, heavily built man, with thick grey hair and a thick, muscular neck, round which his collar and tie rested uneasily, rather as if they did not trust themselves, in that situation, to fulfil their function, knowing that at any moment they might be assaulted by the big hands with the thick, blunt fingers and reduced to absurdity. All his clothes had this appearance, though they were good clothes. Even his shoes looked as if they were resigned to being violently kicked off his feet.

"Yes, Arthur, certainly," Hilda answered. She glanced towards the church. "But perhaps I won't go to the service. We can talk now."

"No, I don't want to disturb you," he said. "I can wait."

"No," she said, thinking that there would be a certain futility in continuing into the church if her mind remained fixed, as it would, on the coming interview. "I'll give it a miss. Where shall we have this talk? Will you walk home with me?"

He seemed uncertain whether or not to agree, then, as if he could not think of anything else to suggest, gave a nod, and as she turned and started walking homeward, he walked beside her.

"It's a long time since we've seen each other," he said.

"Yes," she agreed. "A long time."

"I haven't been able to make up my mind what to do," he said. "I mean, since the engagement. I've thought I ought to see your brother. Something's got to be said. Then I thought perhaps it would be easier if I talked to you first. I thought this way we might be able to avoid trouble. And I don't want any trouble we can avoid, for my boy's sake, and the girl's. She seems a nice girl, I like her. I'd like her and Colin to marry."

He had a strong, deep voice, warmed with a faint touch of the local accent. But he seemed to find difficulty in producing the short, jerky sentences.

As Hilda did not reply, he added, " As things are, it might be all too easy to smash it up."

" But who's likely to want to do that, if you don't? ' she asked.

" You don't need telling."

Her voice rose slightly on a note of anger. " You mean Valerie then! "

" Ah now, let's go at it quietly," he said. " Let's not get angry before we need. We can talk quietly, can't we, at least until we're sure where we stand? "

" So you do mean Valerie."

It confirmed what Hilda had always believed. She had always been sure that the trouble between the two families had been caused by Colin's mother.

For a time Hilda had even wondered if the real explanation of it might not be that Stephen had fallen in love with Valerie. During the short period of intimacy between the two families, he had been particularly attentive to her, putting himself out for her in all kinds of uncharacteristic ways.

" I don't only mean Valerie," Arthur Luckett said, with a roughness which suggested that he had forgotten his own injunction to keep the discussion quiet. " But we needn't go into that now. All we need to be sure about is what we intend to do. The past, thank God, doesn't need to be raked up."

" I wonder if it doesn't."

" Now listen to me, Hilda——! "

"Wait a moment," she said. "Please wait, Arthur. I want you to understand something. I've never—never at any time—understood what the trouble between us was. Nor has Stephen, or if he has, he's preferred not to let me know about it. He's been used, all his life, you know, to treating me as his baby sister. So if you and he had a quarrel, or he and Valerie, you must understand I don't know anything about it."

"Do you mean that?" Arthur asked. "Do you really mean that?"

"Of course I mean it."

He thrust blunt fingers through his hair.

"As a matter of fact, I *did* wonder ... But Lord, that complicates things, doesn't it?"

"What does it complicate?"

"Wait," he said. "Just wait a moment and let me think."

They walked on in silence.

They had left the road and turned on to a path that led down through a wood to the river. Following the path all the way, it would bring them to a gate that led into the Gazeleys' kitchen garden. This way was both the shortest and the pleasantest for Hilda to take to the church and the main part of the village. The wood was a beechwood, the ground under the trees a bronze carpet of dry leaves, the foliage overhead a mingling of tawny shades that brightened to a dull gold where they were touched by the slanting, evening sunlight. Through the thick, greyish trunks of the trees, the river gleamed. The air had the soft, moist fragrance of leaf-mould.

Going ahead of Arthur Luckett on the path, Hilda tried to control her impatience and her growing excitement. But she knew that Arthur was not a man to be hurried, and that if he wanted a chance to think, it would be best to let him have all the time he wanted.

They were almost at the garden gate before he spoke. When he did, however, what he said took Hilda by surprise. He said it broodingly, as if it were only one link in his troubling chain of thought.

"I suppose you knew Stephen's wife quite well, didn't you, Hilda?"

"Amabel?" she said. "Yes, of course."

"She died just before you came here, didn't she?"

"Yes, about six years ago. That's why we moved out here from Ledslowe, you know. It upset Stephen, living in the old house without her."

"I wonder what she was like," Arthur said musingly. "I've often wondered about that. Was she happy with him?"

Hilda turned over in her mind the possible reasons for these particular questions.

"Oh, I see!" she exclaimed. "Katherine's been talking to you about her mother."

"No," he said. "Neither about her mother nor her father. Why should you think she had?"

"Because she always insists that Amabel turned against Stephen before she died."

"And did she?"

"No. That is——" Her voice wavered. "If you want the truth, Arthur—and that means I assume you're going to tell me the truth too—for the last year or so of her life, Amabel wasn't entirely responsible for her thoughts or her actions. Katherine doesn't understand that. At least, I hope she doesn't. We've always done our best to keep it from her. She was away at boarding-school most of the time and didn't see the worst. Amabel drank, you see. And then one day, when she was drunk, she went out and smashed herself up in the car. There —that's the truth about Amabel. But please, please don't tell Katherine."

For a moment he said nothing, then murmured, "Oh God, the poor woman. What was she like—I mean, before . . . ?"

"She was my greatest friend."

The harshness of her tone struck him, and he said quickly. " I'm sorry, Hilda, I don't want to distress you. I'm very sorry. But it's something I've wondered about —what she was like."

They had reached the little gate that led into the kitchen garden. He came to her side, and stood with one hand resting on a gate-post, not intending, it seemed, to go any farther.

Hilda considered whether or not she should invite him to go on with her. Nelson would probably still be painting some way farther down on the far side of the river. Stephen was probably in his study, working or reading. By taking Arthur Luckett through the garden behind the house they could reach the bench against the wall at the end of it without passing Stephen's window, and could go on talking there, undisturbed. Then, at the right moment, Stephen could be called out to join them. It might be the best thing to do.

Her hand went out to the latch on the gate.

" Amabel was very pretty and very gay and would do anything on earth for any living soul," she said. " That's to say, that's what she was like when she was young. We were at school together, and she used often to visit me in the holidays. That's how she and Stephen got to know one another. And he adored her right to the end, though for the last year or two his life with her was terrible. And it's quite untrue that she ever turned against him. She was devoted to him, and touchingly grateful to him for the way he tried to look after her." She pushed the gate open. " Now you'll come in with me, won't you? It's a long time since you've been here, but you've a lot to tell me."

Without moving, he said, " In fact, it was a kind of suicide."

She started. " Is that what you've been told? "

" No, but that's the meaning of what you've told me, isn't it? "

"Yet you *have* been told something! Someone took that simple and tragic story and made something horrible of it—isn't that what happened?"

"It doesn't seem to me a very simple story, Hilda," he said. "I think you left out all the difficult parts."

"Well, are you coming in?" she asked. "Or must we go on walking backwards and forwards between here and the church?"

"Oh, I'll come in, if I may." He followed her through the gate.

They walked through the vegetable garden, then over the lawn, close to the river's edge, then sat down on the bench, with their mingled shadows squatting at their feet.

Hilda saw that the starlings had already arrived at their roost. The small, dark shapes, darting from tree to tree among the ruins, with as much bustle as a homegoing crowd at a London tube station, showed plainly against the broad ribbon of red-gold stretched along the horizon. Suspended above this single band of brightness were some heavy clouds. There was no light yet in Miss Perriman's window.

"Well now," Hilda said, pulling off the small felt hat that she had put on for church and smoothing back her thick, brown hair, "I think it's time you explained the mystery to me. I suppose it's been well meant, this keeping me in the dark, but I'm not sure that it's really been as kind as it was supposed to be."

He sat staring straight before him, rubbing his knees with his big, clumsy-looking hands.

"I suppose it's possible you never knew anything," he muttered.

"Isn't that usually how it happens?" she said. "I believe the victim of a slander is usually the last person to hear of it."

"A slander?" he said.

"Isn't that what's at the bottom of it all? Hasn't

some horrible story been spread around about us, or about one of us? Probably something to do with the death of poor Amabel?"

He turned his head to look at her for a moment, his bushy eyebrows, still black, in striking contrast with his grey hair, lifting in apparent surprise.

"I wonder what's made you think that," he said.

"Am I wrong, then?"

He looked away again. "First tell me something, Hilda. What do you think of my boy? How do you like him? I've told you I like Katherine, but you've said nothing about Colin. I know you've been seeing him. He's told me he's been here several times. But you haven't said anything about him yet."

"Has he suggested that we haven't made him welcome?"

"No."

"Well then——?"

"So you aren't too sure about him. You don't want to commit yourself. What's been the matter?"

"Please, Arthur, you haven't answered my question yet."

"No, because it isn't a case of slander. You're quite wrong there. And since it seems you don't know what happened, I'm wondering if I've actually any right . . ." He brought his hands together suddenly and cracked the knuckles violently. "I'm asking you what you think of Colin for a good reason."

"Then I can only say what I said to Katherine—that I hardly know him."

"What about first impressions?"

"I don't think I trust mine very far. When I think . . ."

"Yes?"

She shrugged her shoulders. "I was only going to say, when I think of how kind you and Valerie were to me when we first came here, and—well, the way one or two other things have happened, it doesn't seem to me that

I can be very good at sizing people up when I first meet them. But still, there's one thing I feel sure about with Colin, and that's that he's very much in love with Katherine. I don't think that he'd ever be an easy person to know, he's so self-contained and guarded, but I haven't any doubt about his feelings for Katherine."

As she ended, she caught herself wondering why she had been unable to speak more warmly of Colin.

His father gave a slight sigh and said, " Well, I don't suppose I know him well either. We haven't a great deal in common. He's got a far better brain than I have, and he'll go a lot further than I'd ever have gone, supposing I'd wanted to. Though it's hard to say these days what one means by going far. Does it mean making a lot of money, becoming famous, or what? "

" What is it that Colin wants? "

" Probably both. Probably everything. Like Valerie. She's always wanted all she could get, poor girl. . . ." He pulled himself up with a catch of his breath. Massaging his knees again, he added, " What I mean to say is, the boy's ambitious, he means to get somewhere, and I mean to help him in any way I can, even though I'm not quite sure where you get to by doing historical research. Perhaps it's just to the sort of life you like to lead. That's what farming's been to me, so I can understand that. But this is a pretty critical time of his life, this remaining year at Oxford. He got a First, and if he does well now, perhaps he'll get straight into the sort of work I suppose he really wants. So he's not to be upset—do you understand that? I won't have him upset or worried." His rumbling voice, which in the main had been quite gentle, sharpened with the animosity that it had already once or twice betrayed.

Hilda's anger flared to match it.

" So now, in a roundabout way, we're getting to it— you think Katherine's going to upset him! "

"No, no, not Katherine. I told you," he said, "I like her."

"Then whom do you mean?"

He frowned. She saw him press his lips together, as if holding back the words that tried to come.

"Do you mean me?" she asked.

He still did not answer.

"You mean Stephen," she said, and suddenly unable to sit still beside him any longer, she sprang to her feet. "Well now, are you going to tell me the reason for that, or aren't you? What harm's Stephen ever done you—or Valerie—or Colin? Even if for some reason you don't like him much, if he offended you somehow, or if you just hate the sight of him without exactly knowing why, in the way one sometimes does... After all, he's a moody person, I know that, and he does sometimes say rather awful things without meaning any harm by it, so if you said that was the trouble, I'd more or less understand it. But all this talk about Colin, who seems to me unusually well able to look after himself, and this suggestion that Stephen or I mean him some harm, well, I—I won't put up with it!"

Her rage, the sight of her with her fists clenched, as if she were proposing to fight him, drew an uncertain smile from Arthur. He stood up beside her. He put a hand on her shoulder.

"I'm sorry," he said. "I'm very sorry I've upset you."

"I'm not upset—I'm just so *angry*!" she cried.

"I've got things all muddled up. I thought—well, I'm not sure if I really did or not—but I suppose I thought you knew the whole story, and so I meant to make an appeal to you to leave the boy alone, and to use your influence with your brother to do the same. I knew that if I tried to speak to him, there'd be trouble, because I didn't even trust myself to keep my hands off him. All the same, things being as they are, that's what I'll have to do, I'll have to see him, and try to talk to him myself. And if you know where he is, I'll do it now. You can stay and listen, if you want to, but I can't—I'm sorry, I find I just can't—pour it all out to you. So if you'll tell me where to find him——"

That was when they heard the scream and the crash.

Afterwards Hilda was never able to tell which she had heard first. Did one come before the other, or had it been as her memory, almost blacked out by the shock, retained it, one fearful and incredibly prolonged sound, which echoed on and on in her horrified consciousness?

But of one thing she was instantly certain, as she and Arthur Luckett, both frozen to rigidity, stood side by side, with his hand lying heavy on her shoulder and their linked shadows printed motionless on the garden wall. It was that the sounds had come from Stephen's study.

CHAPTER V

DISBELIEF made nonsense of all the fears that reeled through Hilda's mind, yet she found herself running. That Arthur Luckett had already leapt towards the corner of the house made that inevitable. She turned the corner to find him at the french window of Stephen's study, trying to pull it open. But the window appeared not only to be closed, but to be bolted inside, and although in the garden it was barely dusk, the long thick curtains were drawn.

"The other door—quick!" Hilda cried.

She thought for an instant that Arthur Luckett had not heard her and was going to smash the window open. But then he caught her arm and pulled her along with him, running towards the front door. This, with a small

porch projecting over it, was near the other end of the
house. Except at night, it was hardly ever locked. But it
was locked now.

Hilda took the lead then, running on round the end
of the house to the back, where another door opened into
a scullery, from which another led into the kitchen.
Neither of these doors was locked, and she had thrust
open the first and was reaching for the handle of the
inner door when Arthur Luckett jostled her aside and
went in ahead of her.

But then he stood confused in the kitchen, not sure
which of the doors ahead of him was the door to the hall,
and when he moved, he made for the wrong one, which
took him into the larder.

Only seconds were lost by this, yet when at last Hilda
and he reached the study together, and saw Stephen
sprawled on the floor, in an impossible attitude, it seemed
to Hilda, that an immensity of time had passed since the
sounds of the crash and the scream had broken in on
whatever Arthur had been trying to say to her.

And the window was wide open now, and the curtains
drawn back.

Hilda flung herself down on her knees beside Stephen.
Arthur, who had given him scarcely a glance, but had
gone straight to the gaping window, turned and said
sharply, " Don't touch him, Hilda! "

Startled, she let one of her hands fall softly on Stephen's
chest, to lie where his heart should have throbbed. That
only a minute or two ago he had been full of life, and
now should be dead, so dead, felt impossible to believe.
Arthur saw her movement and came quickly towards
her.

Because she looked up at him as he did this, she saw
the car go by. She saw only the top of it above the
garden wall, did not see the driver, or anything about the
car except that it was small and grey and driven fast,
yet she felt for a moment that its passing must be of

desperate importance, and stumbling to her feet, she tried to reach the window.

Arthur's arm barred her way.

" Don't, Hilda—don't," he said. " You can't do anything."

" The car," she said breathlessly. " He's getting away in the car! "

" No," he said, " that's just someone passing."

" Let me go! "

She tore herself away from him and ran out into the garden.

By then the car was almost at the bend in the road, too far away for her to read the number. The driver was only a stooped silhouette, seen for an instant.

There was no one else in sight. Once the car had gone, the road was empty. The garden lay still and shadowy in the twilight.

She turned to Arthur.

" If he wasn't in the car, where is he? "

He took her by the arm again and steered her back into the room.

" We ought to telephone at once for the police," he said.

Looking down at Stephen, she did not answer.

Arthur gave a thoughtful look at her white, blank face, and said. " You'd better not stay in here. But I want you where I can keep an eye on you. So wait—wait just a moment, till I've done this telephoning."

He started towards the telephone.

" Why should you need to keep an eye on me? " she said.

" There's a killer loose," he said.

" Is that the only reason? "

She had worked out that the crash that they had heard had been made by the shattering of a big china vase against the metal edge of a filing cabinet, some feet away from where Stephen lay. So it could not have been the weapon that had been used to split Stephen's head open and send him reeling back, to fall with his neck hideously bending on the high brass fender. The vase, she thought, had been the weapon that Stephen had snatched up in a pitiful attempt at self-defence, when he saw his murderer coming towards him.

Suddenly she found herself visualising the scene horribly clearly. She saw poor little portly, excitable Stephen, snatching up the ugly, heavy vase and making a futile effort to throw it, screaming as he threw it, missing, falling, while the other man, some big, strong, calm and deadly man, stood back and watched him die.

A scream began to mount in her own throat. She pressed both hands to her mouth to choke it.

Arthur Luckett, in a gentle voice, was saying, " Yes, Hilda, that's the only reason."

" You saw who was in that car," she said. " You stopped me when I tried to see who it was."

" No, I didn't," he said. "Now I'm going to telephone. Wait just a moment."

He picked up the telephone.

She heard him speaking to the man at the exchange, then to someone at the police station. As he had asked, she waited.

She waited just where she was, but turned her head here and there, looking for what that other man had used to do his murder. But she could see nothing that looked like a weapon that could have taken a man's life. The poker was only a little brass one, and it hung neatly from its usual hook, along with tongs and a hearth-brush, on a small, brass stand. There was no heavy door-stop. The paperweight on Stephen's desk, holding down a heap of letters, was only a small ivory elephant.

Of course, there were a great many heavy books in the room, but these were all on their shelves. Altogether, for a room in which a murder had taken place, there was very little disorder. Poor Stephen could not have put up much of a fight for his life. No chairs had been overturned and nothing but that single vase been broken. He must have been taken quite by surprise, or else been very easily overpowered by someone far bigger than he.

A big figure appeared just then at the window.

For a moment Hilda's stunned senses refused to recognise who it was. She saw the man as Jim Kent, tall, powerful and threatening. Then her mind let go of the illusion, and she said with a stammer of relief, " Nelson! "

He stood there, looking across the room at Stephen with a coldness and detachment of which she had never believed him capable. His tall, usually slack body, outlined against the dusk, was taut and still. If he was aware that she had said his name, he did not show it. He was listening to what Arthur was saying on the telephone. It was only when Arthur put the telephone down and turned, that Nelson stepped into the room.

The two men stood looking at one another with suspicion naked in both their faces. Though she knew that they had never met before, she realised that each knew who the other was.

" You're Wingard," Arthur stated. " A friend of Gazeley's." He made it sound like an accusation. " When did you get here? "

" On Friday evening." Nelson walked forward till he stood over Stephen. His cold, wary glance moved over him from head to foot, then shifted to the fragments of the shattered vase that lay about the base of the filing cabinet.

" I meant here—now," Arthur said.

" You heard Miss Gazeley call out when she saw me," Nelson answered.

He went to her and put his hands on her shoulders. She took a swift step towards him and hid her face against his chest. It was only then that she realised that he was breathing fast and that his heart was hammering violently.

" Which way did you come? " Arthur demanded.

" Up through the wood," Nelson said.

" Then you must have seen——" With a frown, Arthur changed what he had been about to say. " Did you see anyone come out of this room? "

" Only the two of you."

Looking up swiftly into his face, Hilda said, " But you saw a car go by, Nelson! "

" Wait a minute," Arthur said. " I must get this clear. You were coming up the path through the wood from the bridge. You saw us both go out and come in again. But you didn't see anyone come out before us."

" No."

" That means one of two things, then. Either he never left the house this way at all, or else . . ." Arthur stopped. He lifted a clenched fist, as if in sudden rage at himself, and turned and walked out of the room.

" What did he mean? " Hilda asked.

" Or else I'm lying, of course," Nelson said. " But I think there's a third possibility."

He walked to the window, looking out to right and left, thoughtfully stroking his long chin.

" Yes, I think so," he went on. " Certainly, if he'd run my way, I'd have seen him, but if he'd gone the other way, he could have got away through the vegetable garden without my getting a look at him."

" Or he could have got to that car," Hilda said. " You saw it, didn't you? "

" Yes."

" Well, isn't that what must have happened? Didn't he rush out of here, go to the left, only just behind Arthur and me, jump into the car and drive off? "

" But where was the car? " Nelson asked. " Where had he left it when he came in here? When you and

Luckett first rushed to this window, did you see any car in the road?"

She shook her head uncertainly. " I don't remember one. But perhaps I didn't notice. Do you think it's important? "

" I think it's highly important. The driver of that car may be the most important witness in the case—if we can find him. I suppose you didn't see the number? "

" No, I might have, if—if I'd been quicker."

She had almost said that she might have seen the number if Arthur had not got in her way. But even in her stunned condition, something warned her that it was very important that they should all be very careful of what they said of one another. Some quite small statement, some half-sentence, might have unforeseeable consequences.

" Perhaps Arthur saw the number," she said. She looked round. " I wonder where he went."

" To see if the murderer's still in the house, by any chance. Or to see if there are signs that he left it by one of the other doors."

" But if that's what he did," she said slowly, "you'd have seen him, wouldn't you, Nelson? If you'd been coming up the path from the bridge, you'd have seen anyone who came out at the back of the house."

" One would think so."

" So you don't think that happened."

" I don't. But your friend Arthur is going to think it quite probable, because he can't possibly know whether or not I'm likely to be telling the truth." A dry sound that might have been a chuckle ended the sentence. " Perhaps I should warn you that he's not unlikely to think I'm the person who did all the running and dodging, not to mention the murder."

Looking at him incredulously, she saw that behind the deliberately flippant words, there was an extreme tension. She remembered how his heart had pounded as she leant against him. "But you were Stephen's best friend, Nelson."

"Is that what you think?"

"It's the truth, isn't it?"

"Doesn't it take two to make a friendship? And what was the truth about Stephen? Well, perhaps we shall find out now. We shall find out a great many things."

He had been walking, as he said that, across the room to the big desk. As he reached it, he gave a sharp exclamation. His hand went out to the ivory elephant that Stephen had used as a paperweight, and which now straddled a number of papers. For a moment Hilda thought that it was the elephant itself that had caught his attention, then, as Arthur Luckett came back into the room, she saw that it was one of the papers under the paperweight that had interested Nelson.

"Look at this," he said.

He held it out to Hilda. But it was Arthur, coming forward quickly and reaching for it before Hilda could move, who took it from him.

Arthur looked at it expressionlessly, then shrugged his shoulders and handed it to Hilda.

"Does that mean anything in particular?" he asked Nelson.

"It means that poor Stephen took me seriously about something that was meant—well, as a joke of sorts," Nelson said. "And it almost looks as if he was right, doesn't it?"

"I don't know," Arthur said woodenly.

"But you've seen the woman, haven't you?"

"If you mean Mrs. Frearson——"

Hilda stopped him with an exclamation. "It *is* Mrs. Frearson!"

For a moment she was quite certain that it was, that the photograph that she was holding, a photograph, cut from a newspaper, of a woman in black, caught in an attitude of surprise, with a frightened and resentful look on her face, and with one hand coming up to hide it, was indeed a photograph of Mrs. Frearson. But almost as Hilda spoke, she became unsure. There was something wrong about it, apart from the fact that in the way of press-photographs, the picture was so blurred that it would have been difficult for her to recognise in it any but a face really well known to her.

"Is it Mrs. Frearson?" she asked.

"I don't see how it could be," Nelson answered. "I know who this woman is, and she happens to be dead. But perhaps Stephen had persuaded himself that it was Mrs. Frearson."

"He would have liked to do that," Arthur said.

For some reason, this brought Nelson's glance down swiftly to Stephen's body, and then, as if at last that sight moved him, as swiftly away again. He put his hand on Hilda's shoulder.

"Let's get out of here," he muttered. "We haven't got to wait in here, have we?"

He thrust her towards the door.

They went to the drawing-room. Afterwards Hilda remembered that clearly. She remembered walking along the passage, on feet that still obeyed her will, though suddenly they felt as if they did not really belong to her. She remembered a brightness around her, as one or other of the men switched on the light by the door. But as soon as the brightness struck her eyes, darkness closed in on her.

She did not altogether lose consciousness. She knew that they lifted her up and laid her down on the sofa, and that they talked rapidly to one another, and that presently one of them raised her head and poured brandy between her lips. She opened her eyes then, but could not bear the glare of the light and quickly shut them.

"The photograph," she said.

"Yes, Hilda," Nelson answered gently. It was he who was supporting her head.

"Where is it?"

She had been holding it when they left the study, but her hands now lay limp and empty at her sides.

"Never mind about that now," Nelson said.

"Where is it? Have you got it? What have you done with it?" Opening her eyes again, she sat up. For a moment the room tilted dangerously about her, but then grew steady, a neat, ordinary, familiar room, as remote from the room at the other end of the passage as reality from a dream. Only which was the reality and which was the dream? "Where's Arthur?" she asked.

Nelson held the glass to her lips again.

"He's gone to keep a look out for the police, and for Katherine," he said. "You wouldn't like her to walk in on all this, unprepared."

"No." She took a sip of the brandy, then pushed the glass away. "But I don't expect she'll come home yet."

"Where is she?" Nelson asked.

"Out somewhere with Colin, I suppose. And that means she isn't likely to come in till fairly late." She was glancing about the room, on the floor, on the little table near her, on the bureau. "That photograph, Nelson—I was holding it when we came in here."

"It's all right," he said. "I've got it."

"Then I fainted. I don't think I've ever fainted before."

"Haven't you, my dear?"

"And I didn't faint in there, when I found him."

"Then it was delayed shock. Don't worry. And don't worry about the photograph. It isn't important."

Nelson had left her side, and gone to the table where the bottle of brandy stood. He picked it up, poured some into a glass, lifted it half-way to his own lips, then set it down again. His hand was shaking so much that some of the brandy spilled on to the polished table.

Hilda saw it happen and was aware that at any

other moment in her life she would have rushed to the table, to mop up the spirit before it could ruin the polish. That was the kind of thing that she had always done in her other life, the dream-life of peace and security, from which she had been wakened.

"I think that photograph's very important, Nelson," she said.

In spite of his shaking hands, his voice was soft and calm. "Well, perhaps, perhaps."

"You said you knew whom it's of."

"Oh yes."

"Then tell me," she said, her excitement rising again. "It looked just like Mrs. Frearson, except that—except that that woman's hair was fair, that was what was wrong. But you can bleach hair. I think it *was* Mrs. Frearson."

He gave his head a slight shake. "It was a photograph of a woman called Lucy Cater. Does that mean anything to you?"

She repeated the name after him. "Lucy Cater."

She knew at once that it did mean something, that it had even at some time been quite familiar to her, that for some reason it had been familiar to many people, a name in some way famous. She repeated it again, half-aloud. As she did so, memory yielded up the lost image.

"She was a murderess!" she said. "She murdered her husband!"

"She was tried for the murder of her husband and acquitted," Nelson said. "That photograph was taken just after her acquittal. I remember it all very well. And a few weeks later she was killed herself in an accident." He turned his head quickly at the sound of voices outside. "Here are the police, I think. How are you feeling, Hilda? Can you face them?"

She did not answer him. She was staring before her, trying to visualise the face of the fair-haired woman in the photograph, and to set beside it the more familiar though always half-averted face of the dark-haired, lonely woman who walked the river bank at sunset.

"Suppose she wasn't killed, Nelson," she said. "I don't think Stephen believed that she had been."

"Why d'you think that?" he asked.

But before she could tell him, Arthur Luckett and a stranger came into the room.

CHAPTER VI

ARTHUR INTRODUCED the stranger as Inspector Crankshaw.

He was a big man with fuzzy grey hair that stood out erratically round a high, broad forehead. His face was big, with long, loose cheeks and a roll of flesh under the chin. At first glance there seemed to be something rather scholarly about him, but his body was too solidly chunky and disciplined and his small grey eyes had too knowing a look, a glint too raffish, to belong to anyone who had spent most of his life in a study.

He was courteous to Hilda and a little overwhelmingly sympathetic. She found herself thinking of his manner as a kind of clowning, and she suspected that for mysterious reasons of his own he was deliberately presenting himself to her as someone more florid and less educated than he really was. She found him impressive but, particularly in his stagey consideration for her, surprisingly frightening. Of the other men who had arrived with him and who filled the house with their flat, unemotional voices and their tramping feet, she never really became aware.

She had a long talk with Crankshaw later in the evening. One of the other men was present, and seemed to her almost to be competing with the inspector in concern for her, but afterwards she could not even remember his face. Yet for days to come, the image of Crankshaw's, large and sly, with all the expressions that appeared on it so exaggerated that they totally concealed his thoughts, hung hazily before her, never quite fading. It stood for a fear that had entered her heart without her recognising it, for a guilty conviction that in something that she had done or not done, these men would find the cause of Stephen's death.

All the time that she talked to Crankshaw, she worried about Katherine. For a time she thought that something must have happened to the girl, for surely otherwise she would have been home by now. Then on looking at her watch, Hilda saw that it was only eight o'clock, and she did not really expect Katherine much before ten or eleven. Yet her worry continued confusing, her and making her mind wander when she tried to speak coherently to Crankshaw.

She had told him of how she had set off for church, then had met Arthur Luckett and had changed her mind about going to the service, how she had walked back with him, and how they had been sitting talking on the bench in the garden when they had heard the scream and the crash.

Telling him these things, she had suddenly remembered that Arthur had been about to tell her something important when they heard these sounds. Or had he just refused to tell her something? Something about Stephen. He had just asked her where Stephen was, hadn't he? Hadn't he wanted to speak to him?

Muddled and unsure, she fell silent, looking at Crankshaw as if he could put her right about these things, yet feeling that she had probably hopelessly misled him already, because everything that had happened that evening had become so dim and vague.

Out of what she had told him, Crankshaw picked on a point that seemed to her singularly irrelevant.

" Do you go regularly to church, Miss Gazeley? "

" Why—why, yes, fairly regularly," she said.

" Always to the evening service? "

"No, not always."

"But often? More often than not?"

"Well, when we have a visitor staying with us... because then I like to cook in the morning...." She frowned, feeling that it was somehow improper to bring in such a trivial domestic matter.

"And you've got Mr. Wingard staying with you now," Crankshaw said. "Yes, I see. And naturally he, and probably a number of other people—your brother himself, for instance—would have counted fairly confidently on your going out this evening."

"Yes, I suppose so," Hilda said.

"And been very surprised when you returned so soon."

She looked down at her tightly clasped hands. "But that sounds as if you think somebody *planned* to do this."

"That depends. Suppose your brother, thinking you'd be out, asked someone to visit him here, and then something happened between them when that person came."

"But why should it matter to my brother whether I was here or not?"

"Well, if he didn't want you to know that this person visited him..."

Hilda looked up at him stupidly. His big, fleshy face made her think at the same time of a professor and of a bookie, though she was not sure that she had ever in her rather limited life actually met either one.

"Oh, but you're quite wrong—Stephen wasn't like that," she said.

"Like what, Miss Gazeley?"

"Well, I mean he wasn't much interested in women, or anything."

"Not anything at all?"

"No, I don't mean that," she said, getting flustered. "He had lots of interests. He was very interested in his profession. He read a great deal. He—well, what I meant was that he was quite open about it all. You needn't imagine that he was leading a double life."

Crankshaw looked sad and resigned. He looked as if he had heard this statement made over and over again, and knew that it was his fate to go on hearing it made over and over again for the rest of his life, that there was no escape from it, that there was no hope that mankind would ever outgrow this particular folly.

"Everyone has secrets, Miss Gazeley," he said. "I have. You have. There isn't a human being alive who isn't hiding something from his nearest and dearest. And the nearest and dearest won't recognise it. Not if their lives depend on it, they won't."

"I didn't say Stephen hadn't any secrets from me," Hilda said. "Of course he had. He was a solicitor, for one thing. A great deal of his work was confidential. But apart from that, there was nothing there was any need for him to hide. I'm sure of that. We were very close, you see. He could have told me anything."

"That's what they always think," Crankshaw muttered. "They always think they're trusted, simply because they feel so trustworthy. You'd be surprised though... Well, I won't go into that. But if you're right, and you really know as much about your brother as you say, can you tell me why he was murdered?"

Her hands fluttered in a gesture of negation.

As if to himself, he muttered, "I know, I know, he hadn't an enemy in the world."

He leaned back in his chair. He regarded her steadily. He had, Hilda saw with surprise, a slight cast in one eye, and it was this that to some extent gave him his ironic, leering look. To some extent, but not entirely.

"Miss Gazeley," he said, "someone murdered your brother because he hated him, feared him, or wanted something that was in his possession. It was someone your brother was acquainted with, and not someone who'd broken in by chance, because they sat talking quietly together in that room, while you and Mr. Luckett sat outside in the garden. Do you understand that?"

He gave her time to take in what he had said, gave her, indeed, so much time, that it was plain that he did not rate very highly her power to do so.

"Well then," he went on after a little, "we're back where we started. A number of people, your brother included, thought you'd be out. And either your brother took advantage of this fact to ask someone to come and see him, to transact some business which he didn't want you to know about—Wait!" He raised a hand. "I know you don't believe that happened. But it's logically possible. And if it didn't happen, then the other most probable thing is that someone else, who, as you said just now, had planned to kill your brother, chose that time to do it. I admit there are other possibilities, like someone dropping in by chance, and acting on impulse, and all that sort of thing. But I still think one of the first two is much the most likely. So I'd like you, if you can—I know it's very painful for you, and I'm deeply sorry to inflict this on you——" The warm, emotional note returned to his voice. He smiled at her tenderly. "I'd like you to tell me a little more about your brother. I'm sure there's no one who can tell me as much as you can."

Hilda looked away.

"I expect that's true," she said. "I've been living here six years, and, as I said, we were very close. Stephen didn't go out much. He went to his office in Ledslowe, he came home, and usually he'd settle down for the evening with a book, or he might potter a bit in the garden. He was always very quiet, even before his wife's death, though it increased then, I think. She died in a road accident, you know. She——" She stopped herself. There was no need to bring poor Amabel in now. "She died, and so I came here to look after Katherine. My brother sold the house in Ledslowe and bought this one, and we've lived here ever since. Lived very quietly."

"Where had you lived before you came here?" Crankshaw asked.

"In London."

"Then it must have meant a great change for you."

"Oh, not so very," she said. "Before my brother married, I used to live in Ledslowe with him and look after him—and my father too. My mother died when I was quite young, and so I naturally had to learn that sort of thing quite early. But when Stephen married, I thought I ought to leave them alone together, and I'd been trained as a librarian, and besides, I was engaged to be married too.... I'm sorry, I'm wandering from the point. I was very fond of my brother. He was ten years older than I, and when I was little he was very good to me. My father was rather unapproachable, and rather sharp-tempered, and since I had no mother, Stephen——" She sank her face into her hands.

Not impatiently, but in a considering tone, as if he were speaking mainly to himself, to clear his own mind, Crankshaw said, "A widower, faithful to the memory of his wife, not many friends, but such as he had, good ones—that's the picture, then."

She raised her head quickly, grateful that he should have understood, and was shocked to see the irony in his small, sly eyes.

"One of his good friends was Mr. Wingard, wasn't he?" Crankshaw said. "Can you tell me how long it was after you and Mr. Luckett discovered your brother's body that Mr. Wingard came in?"

This rubbed a sore spot of worry in Hilda's mind.

"A few minutes," she said.

"Five minutes?"

"I don't think as long as that. He was coming up through the wood when he saw us both run out of the house. That was the first thing we did, you see. We saw the open window, and we thought that the murderer must have rushed out that way as soon as he heard us at the back door. But Mr. Wingard didn't see him come out, and that made Mr. Luckett think that the murderer must really have waited in the house until we'd come in, then slipped out by the back door. But Mr. Wingard didn't see that either. But he did see the small grey car go by, and I think that's how the murderer got away. I don't know how he got to the car, but I do believe he was in it."

Crankshaw nodded, and she realised that he had heard all this already, probably from Nelson himself.

" Have you considered the possibility," he asked, " that Mr. Wingard wasn't coming up through the wood when he said he was? "

The soreness in her mind, the doubt of Nelson, that had come to her simply because he had been the first person to arrive on the scene after Arthur and herself, made her move uneasily, as she might have moved to allay for a moment a physical ache. But she answered composedly, " You mean it was he who slipped out of the back door when we came in, and then came round the house and found us? But he and Stephen were old friends. Very old friends."

" Didn't they ever quarrel? "

" Of course they did. They were such old friends that they could afford to quarrel. They always made up again."

" I see," Crankshaw said. " So we have a situation where a murderer vanishes into thin air under the noses of three witnesses. That's a very difficult sort of situation, isn't it, Miss Gazeley? If all three witnesses are telling the truth, it's what I should describe as one of the most difficult situations I've ever come across. Now about that press-cutting. . . ."

She was grateful for the change of subject. " Oh, you've been told about that already, have you? I was just going to speak of it. It was lying on my brother's desk, and I thought for a moment it was a photograph of a neighbour of ours, but Mr. Wingard said it's really a photograph of a woman called Lucy Cater."

"Yes," Crankshaw said. "It is. You know who Mrs. Cater was, do you?"

"Yes, Mr. Wingard reminded me. She was tried for the murder of her husband, and acquitted."

"Do you know why your brother should have been interested in her?"

"I suppose just because of her resemblance to someone we know. He might have been—well, sort of amused by it."

"Rather a grim joke. You know she's dead?"

"Yes."

"Did your brother know that too?"

"Oh, I think so."

"He didn't by any chance think he was uncovering a mystery of some sort?"

She shook her head. But as she did so, she thought of the evening when Stephen had returned from London and had joined her in the garden. She remembered the excitement that had possessed him as he watched Mrs. Frearson pass. She saw vividly his small, plump, crouching body.

"I don't know what he thought," she said. "He was a solicitor. He'd believe the evidence. If there's evidence that Lucy Cater's dead, he'd believe it. But—is she dead? Are you sure she's dead?"

Crankshaw nodded his big head.

"Then it must just have been that he was interested in the resemblance to Mrs. Frearson," Hilda said. "Resemblances *are* interesting, and sometimes quite uncanny. Can't you understand that?"

"So she's called Mrs. Frearson?"

"Yes, and she lives in the house over there. . . ." Hilda waved vaguely. "She and her sister, Miss Perriman,

have taken it furnished for a time. The owners, the
Harrisons, are away in South Africa."

" I see. We shall, of course, make certain inquiries. . . .
Now, Miss Gazeley, let me just ask you once more, to be
sure I've got it clear. . . .

And to Hilda's horror, he began all over again, asking
her the questions that he had already asked her.

It put her on the defensive and increased her confusion.
She became convinced that she was not giving him the
answers that she had given him before. Her head swam
and there was a dark mist at the edges of her vision.

The feeling that she had had earlier in the interview
that she had somehow vitally misled him, returned and
filled her with a frightened sense of guilt. He would
catch her out at any moment, she felt sure, and believe
the worst of her. Only there was nothing very bad that
he could believe, for hadn't she been with Arthur Luckett
in the garden, sitting on the bench, when Stephen was
killed? No one could believe that she had had anything
to do with the murder.

As she gave herself this reassurance, she once more
wondered wildly what had become of Katherine. Had
she come home already? Had she come in and no one
let Hilda know? She began to feel angrily sure that this
had happened.

But when Crankshaw let her go, she found Nelson and
Arthur sitting together in the kitchen, which seemed to
be the place in the house most free of policemen, and
when she asked them where Katherine was, Nelson said
that she had not yet come home.

" Don't worry about her," Arthur said. " Colin will
bring her home safely." He looked into her white face.
" I think you ought to go to bed, Hilda. And I'll ring
up your doctor. He can give you something to help you
through the night. Who d'you have? Dr. Barnes? "

" Yes, but I don't want him—not until Katherine's
come back," she said. " I think I'll make some coffee."

"I'll make it," Nelson said, and thrust her into a chair.

She sat there limply for a few minutes, but then Nelson's unfamiliarity with the simple task of making coffee, and his clumsiness in the kitchen, began to irritate her, and she got up, forestalling him in fetching cups from the cupboard and milk from the refrigerator, and in the end it was she who put the coffee on the table and poured it out. The little practical action had made her feel better.

Sipping the hot coffee, she said, " He asked me a lot of questions about that photograph. He asked me why Stephen should have been interested in Lucy Cater. And I didn't really know what to say. Why should he have been interested in her? I said I thought he must just have been intrigued by her resemblance to Mrs. Frearson, but I don't know. Nelson, what do you think? "

" Haven't I often said I didn't know what went on in Stephen's mind? " he answered. " When you've known someone as long as we'd known each other, you stop taking much notice of what goes on inside them. It's pleasant to be able to take all that for granted. When he came to see me in London, he didn't tell me *why* he wanted to know whom I'd mistaken Mrs. Frearson for, he just said he'd like to know that, and I told him without probing into his motives."

" He came to see you in London just to ask you that? " Hilda said in astonishment.

" Well, we had lunch together too. At the time I never thought of those questions of his as his main motive for coming, but now I'm not so sure. He seems to have attached some importance to them, doesn't he? He must have gone to the trouble, after he left me, of getting hold of that photograph."

" I don't understand it," she said. " I suppose it was just curiosity."

She saw a swift interchange of glances between the two men.

"Yes," Nelson said. "Just curiosity."

He had probably intended it to sound reassuring, but his tone was so false that it had the opposite effect. Hilda set her cup down unsteadily.

"What is it you really believe?" she said. "Why did he think that Mrs. Frearson could be Lucy Cater?"

Arthur stood up. He made the movement so abruptly that his chair nearly tilted over behind him. Grabbing it in time, he slammed it back into place with a gesture that looked as if he wanted to smash it. He had looked sympathetic enough a moment before, but now his heavy face looked dark with rage.

At the sight of it, Nelson's face tightened with anger.

"I am sure—*quite* sure," he said in clipped, precise words, "that Hilda knows nothing of the matter—any more than we do."

"I'm not a complete fool," Hilda said. "You do know something, both of you. Or you think you do."

"I'm sorry," Arthur said, and sat down again. "I'm sorry, Hilda. I'm sure you don't know anything. I shouldn't have behaved like that. I'm very sorry."

"It seems to me I know hardly anything about anything or anyone," Hilda said, and feeling that it was useless to try to make either man talk sense to her, she rested her head in her hands and shut her eyes. She opened them again only because she heard Katherine's voice in the passage.

Standing up quickly, Hilda went to the door.

Katherine was in the doorway of the study. Crankshaw was beside her. He had a hand on her shoulder and was giving her one of his heavy doses of sympathy. Katherine's back was rigid, and if she understood or even heard a word that he was saying, she did not show it. But she at once heard Hilda's step behind her, and turning, threw herself into Hilda's arms.

"Come," Hilda said softly. "Come upstairs."

With an arm round Katherine's shuddering body, she led her up to her room.

She found then that Katherine was not crying, as she had thought, but that her eyes were wide and glittering. Hilda tried to make her lie down on the bed, but as soon as the door was closed, Katherine drew away from her and stood stiffly with her back to the window, leaning against the sill.

The strange thing was that, so far as there was any expression on her white face, as she looked at Hilda, it was hatred.

"I know everything now," she said in a low voice.

Hilda started. In response to Katherine's need, she had achieved more control of herself than she had had since the time when she and Arthur had rushed into the study, to discover Stephen's body. But now it seemed that that need had been simulated, and that Katherine, in some rather dreadful way, was completely mistress of herself, a discovery that weakened Hilda, chilling her and bringing back all her confusing terror.

"Think what you're saying," she said. "You don't know—you can't know—who did this."

"It doesn't matter who did it," Katherine said.

"Katherine!" Hilda cried.

Katherine's eyes darted to the door, then back to Hilda. She frowned at her in warning to keep her voice low.

"Colin told me," she said.

"Where *is* Colin?" Hilda asked.

"I don't know."

"Didn't he bring you home?"

"I haven't been with Colin. I've been by myself. I went out with him, but then, when we were having lunch, I made him tell me why he hated Father, and he told me about the way he threatened Mrs. Luckett and tried to ruin her life. So I got up and left. I wouldn't stay with him. I told him he'd made up the whole horrible story himself and that I never wanted to see him again." Katherine's whispering voice had become so hoarse that what she said was barely audible, but with the grimace of hatred still on her face, she went on forcing the words out. " It's all a lie, I told him. But it isn't, is it? And you've always known about it, haven't you? I don't think you liked it. I don't think you wanted him to do it. But you've always known about it."

" I don't understand a word you're saying," Hilda said.

" Or was it too much for you in the end, and did you kill him? " Katherine asked.

Hilda did not answer. As if they had always been bitter enemies, they stared at one another. Then, as she had often seen it happen before, Hilda saw the rage die out of Katherine's eyes and something gentle, though sad and distant, well into them instead.

" Didn't you know—did you really not know? " Katherine asked.

" Know what? "

" That Father somehow found out that Colin's father wasn't Arthur Luckett, and because Mrs. Luckett offended Father somehow, he threatened to tell Mr. Luckett about it—and everyone else. He told her she'd have to treat him differently, or he'd destroy her."

As she brought the last words out, Katherine's soft, dry voice broke and suddenly she threw herself on her knees at Hilda's feet, clutching at her and hiding her face in her lap.

" No, it isn't true! " she sobbed. " It can't be true. I know it isn't."

CHAPTER VII

"OF COURSE it isn't true," Hilda said.

But for some reason she was quite unresponsive to the girl's embrace. She could not caress her or console her.

After a moment Katherine drew away from her. She sat back on her heels, groped for a handkerchief and tried to stop the flow of her tears.

"How d'you know it isn't?" she asked, her voice muffled by the handkerchief, but her streaming eyes watchful.

"Shouldn't I have known of it, if it were?" Hilda said.

"And you didn't?"

"Katherine!"

"I'm sorry." Katherine reached out a hand to her. "But then, what *is* true? Did Colin make it all up? Or has someone been telling him lies?"

"I'm trying to think," Hilda answered.

But she had never felt less able to do so. She kept seeing Crankshaw's face before her, ironic and sly. It made a muddle of every thought she tried to grasp.

As if she were supplying words to come from that face, Katherine said, "I think it could be true without your knowing anything about it. I know there are lots of things about me you don't know. For instance, I don't think you ever realised—you simply wouldn't realise—that I knew all about Mother."

Hilda put a hand to her head. "It isn't true," she said.

"You thought I was too young to know about it," Katherine said. "You kept me at school and thought I wouldn't find out. But of course I did. She got herself drunk and went out and smashed herself up in the car.

She did it on purpose. She did it because she couldn't bear living with Father any longer. And now we know why. She'd found out what he was capable of doing to other people, and she couldn't bear it. Because Mrs. Luckett can't have been the only person he treated like that. If he did it to her, he did it to others."

" It isn't true," Hilda answered, but in a tone that had grown mechanical, for the seed of doubt had sprouted, and for the first time she said to herself that this horrible thing could be true, and that if one accepted the possibility that it was, then it became easy to make sense of a number of things which had always been hopelessly puzzling.

All the same, how could it be true? How could such a thing have happened close to one, and one's eyes been blind to it?

" Tell me just what Colin told you," she said.

" He told me that Father had somehow found out that he wasn't the son of Arthur Luckett, but of a man his mother had had a love-affair with in the early days of her marriage. And Colin said . . . he said . . ." Katherine's voice dried up in her throat.

" What did he say? " Hilda asked.

But Katherine seemed to have gone dumb. She looked at Hilda helplessly, and though she made an effort to move her lips, no sound came out.

" Did he say he felt like killing Stephen? " Hilda said. " Was that it? "

She stood up before Katherine could answer and walked to the window. She put her elbows on the window-sill and looked out into the night. It was a clear night, with a great, white moon shedding an eery brilliance on the straight road running past the house and on the rough pines opposite.

" I don't believe it, I don't believe any of it," she said.

Yet later that night, when the police had left the house, when Stephen's body had been taken away to the mortuary, when Arthur Luckett had gone home and Katherine been induced to take some sleeping-pills and go to bed, Hilda told Nelson Wingard everything that Katherine had told her, and did not say that she did not believe it.

She gave no opinion on it of any kind. She repeated it all in a flat, mechanical voice, and then sat watching Nelson with an expression in her eyes which it was unlikely that he had ever seen there before, an expression which was alert, guarded and distrustful.

Meeting it, he took his time about replying.

" So you want to know what I think about that," he said. " Was Stephen a blackmailer? You haven't used the word, but that's the fear that's in your mind and Katherine's. Yet I can't really tell you till I've had time to consider it. You see that, don't you? And you ought to be in bed now, getting some rest."

" I shan't rest," Hilda said.

" Oh yes, you will. You must. Take some of those pills too and go to bed. You've some bad days in front of you."

" I know. But I want to know what you think about this. You see, Nelson, the whole world I've lived in has suddenly come to an end this evening. I didn't know that till I'd spoken to Katherine. It didn't come to an end with Stephen's death. Not simply with his death. It's come because now I don't know what to think about anything or anyone. It's one's thoughts, isn't it, that make up one's world? And mine's gone, because I don't know what to believe about Stephen, about Katherine, about Colin, about you, or about myself either. Have I really been a blind and stupid woman all these years—so blind and stupid that I've been almost wicked? "

" Don't talk like that, my dear," Nelson answered. " We're all blind and stupid."

" Do you mean you think you've been blind too? " she said. " But you've suspected something, haven't you? I realise now how many hints you've kept dropping, that I chose not to understand. Stephen himself said that about me, you know—that I always managed not to understand anything I didn't want to. He called it a remarkable intellectual attainment."

"It's going rather far to say that I suspected something," Nelson said. "There's a big difference between seeing certain potentialities in a person's nature, and convincing oneself that he ever—well, acts them out."

"But you saw the potentialities. Why didn't I, then?"

"Well, you had to live with them."

"And so you think I blinded myself to them, for my own comfort."

"I meant you were too used to him and too fond of him to ask yourself certain questions about him."

"No, you didn't. All the same, you asked yourself these questions, you saw these—these potentialities, yet you went on being friends with him. Why was that?"

He gave her a long, expressionless look, then turned his head away before he answered.

His words came uncertainly. "I'd known him a long time. . . . And I haven't so many friends. . . . And you were here, Hilda. . . ." His voice faltered, then he went on faster. "And we've all got something in our natures for which we hope to be forgiven. All of us. And we can always be wrong in our estimates of others. Even now, we don't actually know anything against Stephen. You've jumped to conclusions much too fast. It's the shock. But you ought to stop and think before you make up your mind to believe anything so grave."

"I haven't made up my mind about it yet," she said. "But when I think of the way he looked at Mrs. Frearson, that evening after he got back from London, and his having the photograph . . . Nelson, tell me about Lucy Cater. Tell me the whole story. I remember the headlines, but I don't read reports of murder trials."

She thought that he seemed relieved at her questions

taking a different direction, for he settled himself more easily in his chair.

" I've been doing some thinking about that story," he said. " I'm inclined to think it's of no importance to us, except in so far as Stephen may have believed, against all the evidence, that Mrs. Frearson was Lucy Cater, yet there's just a possibility, a fantastic possibility. . . But that's jumping ahead. All the same, if it were true, there'd be a motive for his murder."

" She shot her husband, didn't she? " Hilda said.

" Yes."

" Yet she was acquitted."

" It was accidental, that was the verdict. In my opinion at the time, a correct verdict. I believed her story, which was that her husband had first threatened her with the gun, then when this failed to impress her sufficiently, had held it against his own head, that she'd tried to take it from him and that there'd been a struggle, in the course of which the gun had gone off and Cater had been shot."

" Why should he have wanted to shoot either her or himself? What had she done to him? "

" Nothing, apparently. There was a history of mental instability. Friends testified that he was liable to fits of extreme depression and had tried once before to take his own life. And his dying words, overheard by a neighbour, who'd been summoned at once by Mrs. Cater, sounded as if he were taking the blame on himself. Really it was all quite simple, and the only reason why the case attracted as much attention as it did was the beauty of Lucy Cater, and the fact that a fair amount of scandal about other people came out."

" And then she was killed herself? "

" Yes, in an accident."

" Another accident."

He shook his head at her. " All of a sudden, you're becoming very suspicious, Hilda. It doesn't seem like you. There was nothing mysterious about that accident."

"I don't remember anything about it," she said. "I remember the murder vaguely, but nothing about the accident."

"Well, it was fairly soon after the trial. A few weeks. Lucy Cater was driving from London to York, to stay with relatives or friends, I think. And somewhere on the Great North Road she had a collision and her car overturned and went on fire. She was burnt to death. The driver of the other car was hurt, but not badly, and gave evidence that Mrs. Cater had been driving much too fast, and right in the middle of the road. His story was accepted. For a short time there was a revival of interest in the story of the trial, with a confusion of feelings that, on the one hand, she'd been hounded to her death by people who hadn't believed in her innocence, and on the other, that anyone who drove like that had probably been guilty anyway.... What's the matter, Hilda?"

She was leaning forward, her eyes staring.

"A burning car!" she said.

"Yes, that's how it happened. It's a tragic story." Then as he saw the impatience on her face, he added, "I know what you mean, Hilda. But if it wasn't Lucy Cater in the car, who was it?"

"That's what Stephen must have wanted to know. Who really died in that car, and how did she get there? And isn't that what you meant when you said there was just a possibility—a fantastic possibility—that Mrs. Frearson is Lucy Cater?"

"Yes, but I wish now I hadn't said it."

"You needn't worry. I shan't repeat it, unless I can find out more about it," Hilda said. "And you spoke of a motive."

He stood up and took a few rapid steps up and down the room, coming to a standstill before her.

"If you really won't repeat this, I'll tell you what was

in my mind," he said. " But you must understand I was only letting my thoughts run on, following up certain ideas, which I haven't had time to examine. Suppose it wasn't Lucy Cater in the car, and suppose that she *is* your mysterious neighbour, then it's possible, as you saw yourself, that the woman who died in the car was murdered by Lucy Cater. And if that was what happened, and Stephen got on to it, and if there's any truth at all in young Luckett's accusation that he was capable of a sort of blackmail, who could have a better motive for murdering Stephen than Lucy Cater? "

Hilda started to nod. Everything, she believed for a moment, had been explained, and there was relief in this, a slackening of the strain on her exhausted mind.

Yet what an explanation! What a horror to have to face about her own brother! Capable of blackmail! From eagerness to believe in the guilt of Mrs. Frearson, Hilda passed quickly to a determination to demonstrate that there could be no truth whatever in Nelson's hesitant suspicions.

" Didn't you see her this evening, Nelson? " she asked. " Didn't she go by on her usual walk while you were still on the river bank? "

" No, as a matter of fact," he said, " she didn't."

For some reason, that was worrying. " She didn't? "

" No," he said.

" Are you sure? She slips along so quietly, you mightn't have noticed her."

" She'd have had to pass right in front of me."

" Because if she did go along that path as usual, she couldn't have got across the river and up to the house and done the murder, could she? "

" No, but she didn't go along it. Not while I was there."

Hilda lifted her hands, then let them drop helplessly again. " You don't seem to have seen anything much this evening, Nelson. If only you had. If only you'd seen who came out of the house, or who was driving that grey car, or—or anything." She stood up. "Well, I suppose this isn't doing either of us much good. I may as well go to bed after all."

He did not answer, but, as she turned to the door, stood watching her oddly.

"Good night," she said.

He still did not answer.

She looked round at him, met his curious glance and suddenly realised what she had said.

"I didn't mean anything by that," she said, forcing a smile. "You couldn't see what wasn't there to see. Good night, Nelson."

After a pause, he said, "Good night, Hilda."

She went upstairs to her room.

Undressing quickly, she put on her nightdress and dressing-gown, sat down at the dressing-table and started to brush her hair. For a little while the whole house seemed very quiet, then she heard Nelson come upstairs and go to his room. Meeting her own eyes in the mirror as she heard it, she gave a shrug of her shoulders.

She regretted having said what she had about all the things that he had managed not to see, for of course she had hurt and upset him by saying it. Even more worrying, for the moment, however, than Nelson's being hurt and upset, was the effect that her words had had on herself, for until she had spoken them, she had not really recognised how very blind Nelson seemed to have been for a certain critical few minutes. But now she could not think of anything else.

He had said that he had been coming up the path through the wood when she and Arthur Luckett had rushed out through the french window of Stephen's study. That, Nelson had admitted, he had seen. But he had not seen anyone else come out before them, or anyone come out by the back door. Not that there was necessarily anything strange in that, if, as Nelson had suggested, the murderer, emerging by the study window and keeping close to the front of the house, had made off immediately through the vegetable garden. In that case, only the driver of the small grey car, if he had not himself been the driver, could have seen him. From the path through the wood, Nelson could have seen the back door and the river bank, but he could not have seen the french window itself. He could have seen her and Arthur Luckett only when they were standing by the garden wall, trying to see the driver of the car. But if Nelson had seen them then, they surely should have seen him.

Still steadily brushing the thick brown hair that fell round her shoulders, Hilda tried to remember if she had looked in the direction of the wood.

She thought that she had looked everywhere. Yet perhaps she hadn't. Perhaps she had been thinking too much about the car to look anywhere else. Besides, it had been twilight, and even if she had looked towards the wood, she might easily have failed to see someone standing still among the trees.

Twilight—yes, of course, that was another point. For wasn't it surprising that Nelson should have been out as late as that? He could hardly still have been painting in that light.

Hilda put down her hairbrush, stood up and started to walk about the room.

She wished that she could stop thinking of Nelson and of what he had seen or not seen, but as she walked up and down, she caught herself actually repeating aloud the questions that she had just been asking herself about him, and soon adding others.

Suppose he had seen more than he had admitted, why should he have lied about it? To protect someone else? To protect himself? Was that last the answer? Could that possibly be the truth? Could it be that Nelson had not been on the path through the wood at all, but lurking in the house until she and Arthur had run out into the garden, that he had then gone out by the back door, run swiftly round the house and so appeared at the study window?

But in that case, how could he have known that she and Arthur had plunged straight into the garden? Had he merely guessed it, taking for granted that that was what they had been bound to do? And was it possible, was it conceivable, that Nelson was Stephen's murderer?

Arriving at that question, Hilda stood still, wondering how it could ever have occurred to her to ask it. Then she realised that it was probably merely the first of such questions, and that soon she might be asking the same about everyone she knew. With a shudder, she moved towards her bed, sat down on the edge of it and started to loosen the belt of her dressing-gown.

It was at that moment that she heard the sound from below.

Her first thought was that it was Nelson, that perhaps he had crept downstairs again to fetch himself a drink. Then, as she heard no more, she began to think that she had imagined the sound. But then she heard it again, a soft, sliding noise, like that of a drawer being opened and shut, in the room directly below her, which was Stephen's study.

Tying her belt again, thrusting her feet back into the slippers she had just kicked off, she went quickly to the door and out on to the landing.

"Nelson?" she called.

She had no doubt at that moment of its being anyone but Nelson, and even when there was no answer, she supposed only that he had not heard her. Starting down the stairs, she made no attempt to move quietly, switching on lights as she went, till at the bottom of the stairs, seeing no light shining under the door of Stephen's study, she looked around her and again called, "Nelson?"

As there was still no answer, she went to the door and opened it.

Her hand found the switch by the door and pressed it. In the light she had just time to see that the french window was once more gaping wide, then something crashed on her head and she went down without a cry.

CHAPTER VIII

A BRIGHT LIGHT and a sharp pain were the first things of which Hilda became conscious, she did not know how much later. The pain was in her head. She raised a hand towards it, and a deep voice said softly, " Easy now."

She recognised the voice, or thought that she did, and for an instant wild fear almost drowned her consciousness again. Yet the voice had been gentle.

" Just you lie still," it said. " You'll be all right."

She drew a deep breath, then another. She felt horribly sick.

Like an echo, just behind her, she heard someone else draw a couple of deep breaths.

She struggled to sit up. The movement sent the pain eddying out in circles round her. She was on the sofa, she discovered. Someone had picked her up and laid her down there, putting cushions under her head. Her movement had dislodged one of them and it had fallen to the floor. As she eyed it, a hand, big and brown, with light hairs on the back of it, reached down and picked the cushion up.

She shied away, as if she expected the cushion to come down on her face.

" What are you doing here," she asked.

Jim Kent gave the cushion a shake and dropped it back on to the sofa.

" Looking to see why the lights were on at this time of night," he said. " Lucky for you I did, it seems to me."

" How did you see the lights? "

" I was passing."

" What, at this time of night? "

" That's right," he said. " I was passing—at this time of night—and I seen the lights and the window open. That's all."

He had moved away from her, towards the middle of the room, and turned to look round at her. He was in his working clothes, flannel trousers, a darned pullover and a collarless shirt. His light blue eyes were calm and wary, but his cheeks were taut and pale.

" What was you doing yourself down here? " he asked.

" I heard a noise," Hilda said.

" And come down by yourself to see what it was? "

" Yes, I thought . . ." She began to wonder what she had thought. Something about Nelson looking for a drink.

" That was a clever thing to do in a house where there's been a murder," Jim Kent said. " Next time you'll know better."

Suddenly Hilda remembered having thought that the sound that she had heard from above had been like a drawer being opened and closed. She looked round. She had been right about that, it appeared. Someone had been at the drawers of Stephen's desk. Most of them gaped a little, with the corners of papers sticking up, crumpled and untidy, through the openings, and there was a heap of papers on the floor.

" Someone's been in here, searching for something," she said.

" That's right," Jim said. " It wasn't me, though."

" I hadn't said I thought it was you."

" No, but maybe you'd have been saying it next thing."

" You hate me," she said. " I don't know why, but you hate me."

She saw embarrassment come into the cold blue eyes.

" I was passing," he said. " I saw the light and the window open, so I come in, and there you was, lying on the floor. I don't know how long you been there before I come in."

"I haven't thanked you yet," Hilda said.

She remembered that it was she who had turned on the light in the room, and that in the instant before the blow had been struck, she had seen that the window was open. It was still open, with a chill little breeze blowing into the room, and besides being open, one of the panes had been broken.

"It was good of you to look after me when you hate me," she went on. "All the same, you came in here to hunt for something, didn't you? But someone else—I suppose it was someone else—had been doing the same thing just before you. What were you looking for, Jim? Why couldn't you wait till the morning and simply come and ask me for whatever it was you wanted?"

She saw his big hands, hanging loosely, tighten at his sides, and her fear of him, which she had forgotten for a few minutes, came back to her, telling her that if she had been a fool to come down to this room to investigate a noise, she was being a worse fool to talk like this to a man who was so plainly an enemy.

But his answer was quiet, "It was lucky for you I come in, that's all."

"I wish you'd tell me what you wanted," she said. "I wish you'd tell me why you hate me so. You didn't when you first came to work here."

"No, that's true, I didn't," he said.

"Did I do something? Did I hurt or offend you?"

"No."

"Did my brother do something then? Was that it? But if so, why did you go on working for us? You didn't have to stay, did you? A man like you could easily have found work somewhere else."

"That's right," he said. "Easy."

"Why did you stay, then?"

"Now let's leave that," he said. "Let's say no more about it. It's all done with."

"But is it?"

"Yes, it's done with."

"Jim, if either of us ever harmed you, I'm sorry," she said. "I never meant to."

"Ah, let's say no more about it," he said. "I'm not talking any more than I can help."

"No, you never do," she said. "Yet I remember you used to. When you first came here, you talked about your home and your children. You liked a chat."

His expressionless face flushed. "I said, let's say no more about it. I didn't come in to-night to talk."

"No, I suppose not." Cautiously, because of her dizziness and her aching head, she got to her feet. She gestured at the open drawers of Stephen's desk. "But I'll have to tell the police about all this. Someone got in here. Someone searched the room for something, and knocked me on the head when I disturbed him. It may have been the murderer of my brother."

"I didn't murder your brother, Miss Gazeley. And I didn't knock you on the head or search the room." He walked towards the window. "Are you all right now, if I leave you? Or should I call someone?"

"No, I'm all right."

He stepped out into the garden. But when he had taken a couple of steps, he hesitated, turned and came back to the doorway. He stood there, looking at Hilda. His face was in shadow, and except that he was looking at her steadily, she could make out little about it.

"Look, Miss Gazeley," he said, "we're all right at home, the wife and the kids and me. If you'll just think of that. If you—if you get any other thoughts in your head about us, just think of that."

The faint tremor in his voice made it sound as if he were resisting the temptation to make some more urgent and explicit appeal to her. He turned and walked off.

Wondering what it could be that Stephen had done to him, how he had managed to plant fear and loathing in that strong, quiet man, Hilda stood where she was until she had heard the heavy footsteps die away down the road. Then she went to the window and closed it, turning the key and shooting the bolts at top and bottom. She did it automatically hardly noticing how the broken pane made mockery of her precautions.

Making her way up the stairs, with one hand clutching the banisters and the other her aching head, she thought of knocking at Nelson's door, to tell him what had happened. Then, with full force, all her suspicions of him came back to her, and it no longer helped, she found, to tell herself that Nelson was Stephen's oldest and best friend. For to have been the friend of the Stephen whom she was just beginning to know, seemed in itself a cause for suspicion.

Because of the pain in her head, she took two aspirins when she reached her room, then, leaving on the small lamp by the bed, she switched off the main light and turned back the covers. But at that point, instead of getting into bed, she went, on an impulse, to her wardrobe, opened it and put her hand in to touch the coat that Stephen had given her to comfort her at a time when he had believed that she was hurt and unhappy.

There it was, the fur rich and silky under her fingers. There were tears in her eyes as she went back to bed. Almost at once she fell asleep, and slept till much later than usual next morning.

She was wakened by Katherine coming in with coffee and toast on a tray. Hilda began to protest that this was not necessary and that she had been just about to come down, when she realised that Katherine, standing by the bed, but still holding the tray, was staring at her with frightened fixity.

"Your face," Katherine said aghast. "What have you done to your face?"

Hilda put her hand up to her forehead. There was a swelling, very tender to the touch, just below the hairline. So there was nothing for it but to tell Katherine what had happened during the night, and Katherine at once said that they must have a doctor.

Except that she still had a bad headache, Hilda did not feel too unwell, and would sooner not have had to see the doctor and re-tell her story so soon. But muttering something about the delayed effects of concussion, Katherine rushed off to telephone, and when she returned a few minutes later, she brought Nelson with her, which meant that the story had to be repeated there and then.

As soon as it was finished, Nelson said that this was something for the police, and went out to telephone Inspector Crankshaw, at which Hilda resigned herself to the fact that her day was to consist of telling the same story over and over again.

Katherine had sat down on the edge of the bed. As Nelson left them, she took one of Hilda's hands in hers.

"You mustn't do anything like that again," she said. "You mustn't—promise me!"

"I hope there won't be any occasion to," Hilda said.

"But even if there is . . . I mean, if you hear noises or anything, don't go wandering about the house by yourself and taking stupid risks, because—because you're all I've got now."

"It was very silly of me," Hilda said. "And as Jim Kent said, it was lucky for me that he came by."

"For heaven's sake, it was he who knocked you out, wasn't it?" Katherine said.

"I don't know, I really don't," Hilda answered. "It would be so easy to blame him for everything. But why should he have stayed behind till I came to, when it would have been so easy for him to get away without my having a chance to recognise him?"

"Perhaps you recovered sooner than he expected."

"But somehow he didn't behave as if he'd just made a murderous attack on me that hadn't come off."

"It may not have been a murderous attack. He may not have wanted to hurt you at all. But when you caught him starting to search the room, he must have wanted to make sure that he could finish searching." Katherine stood up. She walked to the window and stood there, turned away from Hilda, so that Hilda could not see her face. Her voice came thinly, with unconvincing casualness. "I suppose he was searching for whatever Father had been holding over him. But you'd think the police must have taken away everything that looked suspicious."

Hilda sighed, thinking that in one thing at least Katherine closely resembled her father. She had the same capacity as he had had for making Hilda feel a hopelessly muddled and slow-witted person, unfit to deal with human problems of the slightest complexity. Both had always seemed to demand help and reassurance from her, and then to impress on her the inadequacy of what she had to offer.

What was it that Katherine really wanted to be told now? That her father could not possibly, by any stretch of the imagination, have been a blackmailer? Or was it possible that she would sooner have been assured that that was just what he had been, so that she could go to Colin and tell him that she knew that he was not a liar, and that she had forgiven him for telling her the truth?

Not knowing how to help, not knowing even what she believed herself, Hilda fell back on silence, as she so often did in dealing with Katherine. This was always, of course, a confession of failure, and its effect on Katherine was generally far from soothing, but at least it made Hilda herself feel safer than when she tried to put her own doubts and confusions into words.

From the stiffening of Katherine's shoulders, as she stood looking out of the window, Hilda thought that some protest at her silence was coming now, some accusation of failure to face facts, of moral cowardice. But if so, this was prevented by the arrival of the doctor. He listened to Hilda's story of the attack on her, examined her and told her to spend the rest of the day in bed.

As soon as he had gone, she got up and began to dress.

Katherine started protesting then, with a good deal of indignation, that there was no point in having a doctor to see you if you would not do as he ordered, and Hilda, for the sake of peace, agreed with everything she said, but went on dressing.

She had just gone downstairs and started to wash up the breakfast things, when Inspector Crankshaw arrived.

She had to endure the load of his sympathy before he would let her tell him her story of the night before, but then he made her tell it three times. Not that he asked her directly even once to repeat it, but he varied his questions in such a way as to draw the facts from her over and over again, and at the end offered no comment whatever, except that he was very sorry for her, very, very sorry.

" And now," he said, " there's just one other thing I'd like to ask you."

Nearly frantic at the sound of her own voice, Hilda thought of telling him that she would not, for any reason whatever, tell that story to anyone ever again. But in meeting the knowing little eyes in his large, fleshy face, she had the same feeling as she had had the day before, the feeling that she had somehow vitally misled him, and this left her, when it came to the point, unable to defy him.

It was a relief, therefore, that his question seemed to be on a different subject.

" Do you happen to know, Miss Gazeley, if your brother telephoned Mrs. Frearson or her sister yesterday morning? " he asked.

" No, I'm sure he didn't," she said.

"You're sure? You mean you have certain knowledge that he didn't?" Crankshaw asked.

"Well, not exactly. I mean, I suppose, why should he have telephoned either of them? Have they said that he did?"

"On the contrary, they both deny it. But the operator at the telephone-exchange said that she put a call through from this number to Mrs. Frearson's, at about nine o'clock in the morning."

"Suppose she did, what would that mean?" Hilda asked.

"I don't know."

"About nine o'clock? I'd probably have been in the kitchen, getting breakfast. I shouldn't have heard if anyone was speaking on the telephone."

"I see. Well, I was hoping you might be able to help me there, but it can't be helped. That's life, isn't it?"

His easy acceptance of her inability to tell him what he wanted to know seemed to her quite false, his good-humoured smile quite hypocritical. This made her want to explain and elaborate.

"It could have been Stephen who telephoned—I mean, if somebody did," she said. "Perhaps he wanted to say something about that photograph, though it would be a strange thing to raise on the telephone, with someone you hardly know at all."

"Just what I thought myself," Crankshaw said. "So I wondered, mightn't he have been asking her to come and see him to discuss it—in the evening perhaps, when she'd be taking her usual walk in this direction anyway, and you'd be at church?"

"Asking her to come *here*?"

"That's what I wondered. But I seem to have been wrong, because Mrs. Frearson says, first, that he never telephoned her at all, and secondly, that she never walked this way at all yesterday, because she spent the whole evening in Ledslowe with a friend."

"I didn't know she had any friends in Ledslowe," Hilda said. "She's always been alone, whenever I've seen her."

"Yes, that's what I've heard from other people too," Crankshaw said. "But she spent yesterday evening at the Three Pigeons with a man called Stanley Brown. Curious, really. You wouldn't know him, but he happens to be rather well known to—well, to us."

"Good gracious!" Hilda said.

"And there's no doubt about it," Crankshaw said. "She did spend the evening with Brown in the Three Pigeons. Half a dozen people noticed them. And before that she ate fish and chips with him at the Regent Café."

"Why is he, this Stanley Brown, known to the police?" Hilda asked.

"For having committed most of the crimes in the calendar. Petty crimes, you know. I'll say that for him, he doesn't aim high, he isn't ambitious."

"And Mrs. Frearson spent the evening with him?"

Hilda saw the raffish glint that she found disturbing in Crankshaw's little eyes as he turned to the door.

"Just life again," he said. "Always surprising, even when you're used to it."

He went out.

It did not help Hilda to sort out her feelings then that, only a minute or two after he had gone, Katherine came in, bringing with her Miss Perriman.

CHAPTER IX

Though Miss Perriman began with condolences, they were abrupt and merely formal. She was less capable of hiding her own feelings than she probably believed herself to be, and the feeling that showed far more plainly than sympathy on her square, weather-beaten face was anxiety, at its most intense and painful.

A few days before, this might have escaped Hilda's notice. She had preferred to accept people as being more or less what they wanted her to think them, for this had helped to make life calmer and friendlier than it might otherwise have been. But the murder of her brother and the knock on her own head had sharpened her perceptions. Before Miss Perriman had spoken a dozen words, Hilda had recognised the evasiveness of her eyes and the restlessness of her big, brown, powerful hands.

Sitting down and kneading her prominent knuckles together, Miss Perriman said earnestly, " I'd like to help, Miss Gazeley, if there's anything whatever I can do. Not that I suppose there is—there never is, just when one would most like to be of use. But if there *is* anything, I mean, anything whatever... I've had my own troubles, you see. I know what it is to face—well, things. But at least, you aren't alone, are you? It's always much worse if one's alone."

" No, Katherine and I are together," Hilda answered.

" I was really thinking of your friend, Mr. Wingard," Miss Perriman said. " He's staying with you, isn't he? I saw him down by the river as I came along. He must be an immense help to you both. I was so glad to see him painting away just as if nothing had happened. That's the kind of friend one wants around when frightful things happen to one. Nice, calm, detached people."

Remembering now that she had not seen Nelson since she had come downstairs, Hilda looked questioningly at Katherine.

" Yes," Katherine said, " since early this morning. That's where I had to fetch him from when I brought him up to see you."

" And it shows he's a true artist," Miss Perriman said.

" That's to say—well, I don't actually know a thing about it, but that's the sort of thing people say about artists, isn't it? When they're really upset, they bury themselves in their art. Probably Mr. Wingard couldn't sleep, and went out as soon as it was light. You or I would just have lain there, tossing and turning, but he, lucky man, would have started thinking of painting. I hope he's staying on with you for a while. He isn't going straight back to London, is he? "

The question had a queerly familiar sound. Though Miss Perriman had not asked precisely that question before, she had, at tea in her own house, asked others so like it, probing obliquely for information about Nelson, that what she said now seemed almost a repetition. On that occasion Hilda had pretended not to notice, but now she turned again to Katherine, and with acid in her tone, said, " I think it's time that Miss Perriman met Nelson, don't you, Katherine? They may have quite a lot to say to each other."

" Ah, I didn't mean you to disturb him," Miss Perriman said quickly, as Katherine, with an understanding nod, went out to fetch him. " I just wanted to make sure you wouldn't be alone. Even two women together, that isn't the same as having a man around. I'm used to it, of course, but at the present time . . ."

Hilda interrupted, " Miss Perriman, I'm very tired. I don't feel very well. I simply haven't got the strength to beat about the bush. I'm sure you can understand that. I know you didn't come here this morning to tell me how sorry you are about my brother's death. You came to find out if there's any special danger threatening your sister. Well, I don't mind your doing that. We all know there's a mystery about her. We all know you spend your time trying to protect her. I only mind your not coming straight to the point about it."

For a moment the other woman said nothing, then she let her fidgeting hands drop into her lap. Lying palm upwards on her rough tweed skirt, they looked as if they had just let go of something. A small, discouraged smile slightly relaxed and softened her rather granite features.

"I'm sorry," she said. "I suppose I'm a lot stupider than I like to think. So you all know there's a mystery about my sister, do you? Yes, of course you do. I needn't pretend I didn't know that. But deception's a bad habit. It grows on one like a drug. One becomes practically incapable of getting along without it. And perhaps the worst part of it is that one deceives oneself all the time that one's successful in deceiving others. If they don't actually call one a liar to one's face, one's perfectly happy. I never expect people to distrust me, you know. I always believe my own underlying honesty must be so obvious to everyone that they'll swallow anything I want them to believe—because I really *am* honest, you see. I mean, my intentions are honest. I mean well. I'm only trying to do my best all round. But I'm afraid I'm very stupid."

She stood up and walked to the window. A heavy, slouching figure, with her big hands locked behind her, she remained there, staring out into the garden.

Hilda, who felt at first that she ought to say something kind in response to this speech, although she had only half understood it, soon began to feel that really it would be better to say nothing at all. For suspicions were things which she still did not know how to accommodate in her mind. They blocked it as Miss Perriman's wide shoulders were blocking the light from the window. So it would almost certainly be wisest to wait for help, to wait for Nelson.

When he came in and was introduced to Miss Perriman, he showed distinct signs of embarrassment, actually making a remark about the weather, with which Miss Perriman, abruptly perching herself on the arm of a chair, like an ungainly schoolgirl, absently agreed. Her glance was less evasive now, and instead of darting here and there, fixed itself brilliantly on Nelson's long sombre face.

She said challengingly, " The police came to see us this morning, Mr. Wingard."

" So I had heard," he answered.

" They asked us about a telephone call we're supposed to have received from this house yesterday morning."

" But didn't you receive it? " he asked.

" No," Miss Perriman said.

" But I thought the information came from the exchange," he said.

She gave an abrupt laugh. " Don't tell me you think our local exchange is incapable of making a mistake."

" I'm afraid we're all capable of making mistakes, Miss Perriman."

Anger sparkled in her eyes. " And I'm making a mistake, denying that that call was made—or, at any rate, answered? Well, I absolutely deny having answered it myself, and when my sister also denies it, I believe her." She shot a sharp and rather hostile glance at Hilda. " Miss Gazeley will tell you I came here to talk to you about my sister."

Nelson had sat down, and was groping for his pipe in his pocket. Bringing it out, he frowned at it, put it away again, and said, " I'm afraid I owe your sister an apology. If the police have been bothering her, it's probably all my fault. But I never intended it. I'm truly sorry." He turned to Hilda. " You haven't explained? "

She shook her head.

Katherine at that moment gave a sharp sigh, as if she were in a state of tension that was almost more than she could bear.

All three looked at her.

Her cheeks reddened. " It wasn't your fault, Nelson. It was my father's. I was there when you told us about how you'd mistaken Mrs. Frearson for someone you knew —for someone who was dead. And I remember quite clearly, he was sitting there. . . ." She looked at the chair on the arm of which Miss Perriman was sitting, with one foot swinging. " And he was fearfully interested at once. You couldn't have expected that, so it wasn't your fault."

" It doesn't matter much whose fault it was," Miss Perriman said. " What matters is my sister being upset by being asked a lot of questions that she didn't understand. She's had a bad time, you know. She's been very ill. And I've had a fairly bad time too—I'm not complaining about it, but I assure you it hasn't been easy— trying to get her back to normal. So all I'm worrying about is that she shouldn't be bothered any more. I don't care who started it in the first place."

" I understood from Inspector Crankshaw," Hilda said, " that Mrs. Frearson had a perfect alibi for the time of my brother's death, so I don't see why she should be bothered any more."

A dark flush came to Miss Perriman's face. Her hands had grown restless again, the fingers twisting and untwisting in a variety of complicated knots.

" And you think there's something peculiar about that alibi, do you? " she said. " Something suspicious? Well, let me tell you, you don't understand my sister. I've been trying for weeks to get her to mix with other people. I've begged and implored her to meet some of the nice people I've got to know since we've been here. She'd never even listen. She'd just slip away like a shadow and go for a walk by herself. But yesterday evening she came home looking—well, it took my breath away. There was colour in her cheeks. She was gay, like a child who's been to a party. She said she hadn't had such fun for years and she told me all about spending the evening with this man Brown. And I realised at last that all this time I've been trying to do the wrong thing for her, because really that's the sort of thing she's used to—pubs and picking up people and so on. That's the sort of life she lived with her husband, going out every evening, drinking too much and mixing with all sorts of people. I never liked it, I never thought it was good for her, I hoped this was the time I could save her from it. But I've been quite wrong about it all, I see now, because half her trouble for a long time is just that she's been desperately bored—and afraid of upsetting me by admitting it, of course, because she's wonderfully grateful for what I've tried to do for her. So you see, there's nothing suspicious about her alibi at all—only a bit scandalous, which is quite another thing." She got up from the arm of the chair, and as if it helped her to dismiss the problem of her sister's behaviour, gave her big body a shake, like a dog shaking water off its coat. "I only wish mine were as good."

"Isn't it?" Nelson asked.

"Oh no, I haven't one at all," she said. "Not a shadow of one. I was in the garden, doing a little weeding, that's all. And I don't even know for sure when I started or when I stopped. I went out some time after tea, and it was so pleasant I stayed out until the light began to fade. I remember watching an enormous flock of starlings fly overhead. I rather dislike birds, really, but they looked quite wonderful, flying into the sunset. However, I can't expect them to corroborate what I've told you."

Nelson had been groping for his pipe again. Holding it cupped in one hand, he said, "Well, I repeat my apologies, Miss Perriman. In so far as it's my fault that the police have troubled you and your sister, I'm very sorry. And would you please apologise to your sister for me, if I startled her a few weeks ago when I took her for somebody else."

"She told me about that," Miss Perriman said. "She couldn't understand it and I think at the time she was rather frightened, but she's forgotten all about it by now."

She stood up and held out a hand to Hilda. " You were wrong a little while ago when you said I didn't come here to say how sorry I was to hear of your brother's death. I did want to say it. But it's true there were other things I wanted to say too. I did want you to understand about my sister and that there was nothing —nothing at all odd about her spending the evening with that man Brown." She turned to the door.

Hilda, who saw her out, then came back to the drawing-room, meaning to point out to Nelson something in Miss Perriman's behaviour that had struck her as very strange, found Katherine already excitedly talking about it.

". . . And she never asked once whom you'd mistaken her sister for," Katherine was saying. " In fact, you'd almost think she didn't want you to have a chance to tell her. And d'you know what I think that means? I think it means she knew all along, and that Mrs. Frearson *is* Lucy Cater."

" That's what I think too," Hilda said. " I'm sure she's Lucy Cater."

" Poor woman," Nelson muttered.

" Mrs. Frearson? " Katherine said. " But if she's Lucy Cater, she's probably a murderess."

" No, Miss Perriman. Poor frantic woman. She was lying, of course."

" About her sister's alibi? " Hilda asked.

" No, about her own."

Hilda did not understand that.

" How do you know? " she asked.

Nelson had started to fill his pipe at last, but was being so slow about it that there might have been some brake on the movement of his fingers.

" She lied," he said thoughtfully, " and very clumsily."

" She's rather a clumsy creature altogether," Hilda said.

"But Mrs. Frearson *is* Lucy Cater, isn't she?" Katherine said.

"Well, as you said, if she is, she's probably a murderess," Nelson said in the same measured way. "She probably murdered the woman whose body was found in her car." He struck a match, but let it burn out without trying to light his pipe with it. "Unless that whole affair was arranged by Miss Perriman. There's something rather dreadful about her devotion to her sister—or doesn't that strike you?"

"It strikes me," Katherine said. "An awful sort of possessiveness. I've thought from the first there was a lot of the gaoler about her. And of course if she had done a murder for her sister, to help her sister disappear, she'd have her completely in her power ever after."

With a wry smile, Nelson said, "We're going a little fast, perhaps. And among ourselves that doesn't matter, but I don't think we ought to speak of it to anyone else. And I mean, not even that young man you're engaged to, Katherine. Can you keep secrets from him, or does that seem to you immoral?"

"I'm not engaged to anyone," Katherine said. She gave Nelson one swift look as if she hated him, then walked out of the room.

Nelson looked after her in dismay.

"What a fool I am," he said. "But you don't need telling. We'll have to do something about that, Hilda."

But Hilda did not want to have to think of too many things at a time. Katherine was one problem, Miss Perriman and her sister were another. And Nelson himself, she must remember, was yet another.

Closing the door that Katherine had left open, and returning to stand near the fire, Hilda said, "What was the lie Miss Perriman told about her own alibi, Nelson?"

"She wasn't in her garden when she said she was," he told her.

"How do you know?"

"Well, I don't think she was," he said. " So perhaps she was near here. I wonder...." He struck another match and this time sucked the flame down into the bowl of his pipe.

"You didn't see her, did you?" Hilda said.

He raised his eyes to hers. " Still thinking of all the things I didn't see as I came in from the river?"

"I suppose so," she said unhappily.

"That's what I'd be doing, if I were you," he said.

"It's just—it's just that it's all so impossible.... All of it." She rested an elbow on the mantelpiece and her aching head on her hand. " Last night I started having all sorts of doubts about you, and I made up my mind then that the best thing would be to tell you all about them. For instance, why did you stay out there so long after the light had gone? Then, why didn't I see you coming up the path from the wood when Arthur and I ran out into the garden after we'd found Stephen? Then, why hadn't you seen Mrs. Frearson go by? But of course we know that now—she didn't go by. And I suppose the other answers are equally simple."

He smiled at her. " You're a nice person, Hilda. I'm glad you said it all. Now let me think. I stayed out there by the river long after I'd stopped painting, for two reasons. It was a nice evening and very peaceful and pleasant there, and also—this may have occurred to you—I thought I'd like to have another look at Mrs. Frearson. Really that was just from curiosity. But she'd haunted me somehow, ever since I'd seen her. Only she didn't come, and so at last, when I was sure it was too late for her, I crossed the bridge and walked up through the wood. And then I saw something——" He broke off with a laugh. " I *thought* I saw something," he corrected himself, " which made me stop dead in my tracks. I thought I saw you and Arthur Luckett standing side by side in front of that bench at the end of the house, and I thought Luckett had his arm round you. And then you seemed to break away from each other and go racing off round the house. I think I was just about as surprised as I've ever been in my life, not to mention embarrassed, and of course I had an idiot impulse to rush madly to your rescue and at the same time to turn round and walk very quickly in the opposite direction. And torn between the two, I stayed just where I was, until I saw you and Luckett appear at the back of the house, go in there and a moment afterwards rush out from Stephen's room. About then I began to realise that something of a quite different sort was wrong."

Hilda had been listening incredulously.

"But Nelson, Arthur and I never——" She stopped with a small quaver of laughter. "No, no, I'm wrong! We *were* standing there, and just before we heard the scream and the crash Arthur had put his hand on my shoulder. But it wasn't exactly a passionate gesture. He was saying he was sorry he'd upset me—just trying to be kind."

"I know," Nelson said. "When I'd got over my surprise, I realised the scene I'd witnessed hadn't been one of high emotion. All the same, it's why I was still lurking among the trees when you came running out of Stephen's study."

"Well, I think that's just about the one complication between the Lucketts and us that nobody else has ever thought of," Hilda said, finding herself thinking that this oddly mistaken view of herself and Arthur Luckett placed Nelson very certainly among the trees, where he had said that he had been at the time of the murder. But still a nagging little worry about him remained in her mind. "And you didn't see anyone else near the house—anyone at all?" she asked.

"No, I didn't."

"But you did see the little grey car go by."

"Yes, I told you I saw that."

"Only not who was driving it."

"No."

"Well, there we are then—not much further on." She went towards the door. But then she turned back to him and said, "Aren't you really rather angry with me, Nelson, because of my doubts?"

"I'd always find it difficult to be angry with you, Hilda."

Giving her head a dubious little shake, she went out, and as she walked along the passage, thought suddenly that it was time for her to do something about getting the lunch.

For a moment it seemed curious to be thinking of something so ordinary, but then she discovered that it felt pleasantly steadying. Cold roast pork, she thought, and salad, and the remains of yesterday's apple tart. That would be nice and really no trouble at all.

Yet first of all, before fetching any of the food out of the refrigerator, she thought that she would like to sit down quietly by herself, for it seemed to her that ever since she had woken up that morning, someone or other had been talking to her, and that was an experience to which she was almost as unaccustomed as she was to murder. To sit down somewhere alone now, and to refrain if she could, from thinking of anything in particular, would be wonderful. So would a cigarette.

But she smoked so rarely that she had no cigarettes of her own. The only cigarettes in the house, unless, of course, they had been removed by the police for their own mysterious purposes, would be in Stephen's study.

Going to the end of the passage, she opened the door.

A man was bending over one of the open drawers of Stephen's desk, staring down at the tumbled papers inside it. Hearing her come, he turned slowly and smiled at her.

CHAPTER X

It was his calm that unnerved her. If he had looked in the least alarmed or guilty, she might have known how to make some effective and reasonably dignified protest. As it was, she was not far from apologising for having interrupted him, as she had so often apologised to Stephen, when some household matter had brought her to that door.

Colin Luckett did not offer any apology. He merely stood before the desk with his hands hanging loosely at his sides, and murmured a normal greeting. Hilda noticed that the heap of papers thrown out of the drawer by the searcher of the night before was still on the floor.

In a voice that came out on a far shriller note than she had intended, she said helplessly, " It's so stupid! There's nothing there! The police took away everything that could be of the slightest importance."

" That's something that had occurred to me," Colin answered.

" Then what are you doing here? "

" Nothing in particular," he said.

She was almost hypnotised by the quiet self-assurance in his blue eyes into accepting this as an adequate explanation of his presence. But then it came to her that this self-assurance could not possibly be real. How could it be? It must simply be a look that he could produce on his handsome young face when he felt that he needed it. Behind it, if he were human, there must be nervousness and uncertainty. Only perhaps he wasn't human. She had never felt quite sure of it.

" So you didn't have time to finish last night? " she said.

He showed a mild perplexity.

She went on, " Wasn't it you who broke in here last night? Wasn't it you who hit me on the head and then got frightened away by Jim Kent before you could finish the job you came to do? "

For an instant she thought that he looked as shocked as he ought to have looked from the start, but since he turned away from her, stooping and carefully closing the drawer in which he had apparently been searching, she was not sure if the distress that she thought that she had seen in his eyes had really been there. What she did recognise in them, when he looked up at her again, was a new wariness.

" I've never to my knowledge knocked anyone on the head since I left school," he said. " And even then I remember it took a certain amount of provocation to make me do it. I've always been a quiet type."

She came farther into the room and closed the door behind her.

" Do you want me to think you don't believe it happened? " she asked. " It did happen and I've still got a very nasty headache."

" I'm sorry," he said.

" Sorry! " At last she was beginning to lose her temper. " That's a wonderful way to apologise."

" It wasn't exactly an apology," he said. " I'm just very sorry you've got a nasty headache. But at a time like this it might be rather dangerous to start apologising for what one hasn't done. The truth is that this morning is the very first time I've broken into your house. It really is."

" Well, don't you think you might bring yourself to apologise for telling Katherine the sort of things about her father that you did yesterday? "

She was satisfied to see a flush creep into his cheeks.

" Didn't somebody have to tell her? "

" Do you know she's saying this morning that you aren't engaged any more? "

"I didn't know it, but it doesn't surprise me."

"Haven't you telephoned her or tried to see her?"

"No."

"Well, a wonderful husband you'd have turned out, if she hadn't decided to break off the engagement!" Hilda said. "A real strong shoulder to lean on in time of trouble?"

"But she doesn't want to see me."

"What makes you think so?"

"She told me so. Besides, how—how could she?"

To her surprise, in that last sentence, the level voice had faintly quavered.

Hilda sat down. It gave her a little time to think out what to say next. For here again, she realised, something might not be as she had imagined. It could be that Colin's composure was only a thin shell, a fragile cover for other very different feelings.

"You mean, after the things you'd said to her about her father?" she said.

He answered quickly, "I didn't want to say any of it. And if I'd known what she'd got to come home to in the evening, I shouldn't have—ever. But I'm not trying to justify myself. I wish I hadn't said it, but I did. Perhaps I even half-intended to let her drag it out of me. I don't like to think about that. And I don't really expect her to forget it."

"All the same..." Hilda was frowning at him, not any more in annoyance, but in sheer uncertainty of how to treat him. "Suppose you tell me what you were hunting for here, Colin."

He shook his head. "I wasn't actually hunting for anything."

"You know Katherine told me what you'd told her—or some of it—about your mother and——" She stopped, seeing that his face had gone dead white.

"Naturally," he said with a tight-lipped smile.

"Yes, it *was* natural, so don't sound so superior about

it," she snapped at him. " Did you expect her to carry all that load by herself? "

" I had a queer sort of idea she might share it with me," he answered aloofly. " But that didn't work out. You're quite wrong, though, if you think I hold it against her. I'm the only person I'm blaming at the moment."

" Except, of course, my brother."

" Well, perhaps we'd better not talk about him."

" Only it's difficult for me not to talk about him," Hilda said. " After all, it's you who seem to have started the story that he was a blackmailer, and this is the first chance I've had to discuss it with you. And there are quite a number of things that I want to ask you about it. For instance, how long have you known it? "

" I never actually called him a blackmailer," Colin said. " And why is it important how long I've known about it? "

" Because I want to know if you already knew about it, knew that my brother's supposed to have tried to blackmail your mother, and the reason for it, before you asked Katherine to marry you."

He eyed her dubiously. " I wonder what's in your mind. Do you think I didn't know, and so, once I'd found out, must just have been waiting for a chance to smash up the engagement—or that I did know all along, and so could only have been pretending all this time to be in love with her, as part of some scheme of vengeance on your brother."

" I don't *know* what's in my mind! " Hilda cried. " I just want to know what happened—and when—and how! "

" Well, take your pick," he said. " Those are both plausible answers, aren't they? "

" Only when you say that, you make them both sound absurd."

" Then at least that's a step in the right direction."

" I'm not at all sure of that," she said. " Always, from the start, you looked at my brother as if you hated him, and also as if you were waiting—waiting for him to do or say something. . . . Oh, I don't know what it was, but I think you must always have had this idea about him."

" And so I couldn't possibly have fallen in love with his daughter, although she's . . ." Again the calm voice quavered. " Although she's Katherine? "

Hilda twisted her fingers, wishing for an instant that it was not such a long time since she herself had been in love with anyone.

" I'm sorry, Colin. Probably I'm asking all the wrong sort of questions. But I do want to know—I must know—just what you think my brother did to your family. Because if what you think is true, I'll have to try to undo it somehow. Not that it would really be possible, but I could pay back anything he took from them. On the other hand, if it isn't true . . ."

But she felt so little hope now that it could turn out not to be true, that she did not trouble to say what, in that case, she would demand of the Lucketts. She had only to remember the evening when she and Stephen had sat together in the garden and seen Mrs. Frearson go by, and to recall Stephen's face then, taut with what she now thought of as the exultation of a hunter sure of his prey, for her to abandon the pretence that Stephen could not be capable of blackmail.

Colin did not answer immediately. Then he said, " All right, I'll tell you what I can. I'll tell you what my mother told me. But there's no question of paying anything back. Nothing was ever paid. When your brother threatened her with exposure, she decided at once there was only one thing she could do, and that was to tell my father everything herself. So she did, and that was the end of the matter. Apart from that . . ." He put out a hand in a tentatively friendly gesture. " I know you didn't know anything about it. I've told Mother so."

" Only perhaps she doesn't quite believe you," Hilda said.

" Father does, anyway."

" Since when? He wasn't quite sure about it yesterday."

" Yesterday? " Colin said.

" Yes, he was here—we were out in the garden, talking about all these things—when we heard the noise in here, the crash and the scream. Didn't you know that? "

" I knew he was here when you discovered the murder," he said.

" Well, he'd been telling me he wouldn't have you upset. I didn't understand what he was talking about and I said so. He didn't seem able to make up his mind whether or not to believe me. But in a way, you know, I still don't quite understand, because he was speaking, it seems to me, as if he thought you didn't know anything about these things either. I mean, it was as if he was trying to persuade me—me and Stephen—not to upset you at this point in your career by telling you just what you've been telling me yourself."

Deep lines appeared on Colin's face as she said this. They slanted down from his nostrils to the corners of his mouth. Hilda knew at that moment how, if life were unkind to him, he might look when he was forty.

" He didn't know I knew," he said.

" But how's that possible? "

" Because I only found out yesterday morning."

Meeting her shocked look, he gave a hasty shrug.

" Yes, I know—and I went straight to Katherine with my troubles. Spineless, wasn't it? " The lines had faded already, leaving him looking younger than usual, with an unfamiliar air of awkwardness and confusion. " I'd always known, of course, that there was trouble between our families, but I didn't know what it was, and when I first met Katherine it made her, somehow, seem all the more attractive. Montague and Capulet stuff, you know. Then, when we started going about together, my mother told me she didn't like it. She said Mr. Gazeley was a bad man, a really bad man. But she only managed to make it sound rather absurd and melodramatic. I know she can be rather hysterical sometimes, you see. I know she exaggerates. Then Katherine told me about her mother's death and how she believed her father had caused it, though she didn't seem to know how exactly, and I thought it must have been something to do with that that my mother had been talking about. I used to look at him—I think that's what you noticed—I used to look at him and wonder what he'd really done. Then yesterday my mother told me what he'd done to her. She told me "—his voice suddenly became hoarse—" told me that in the early days of her marriage she'd had a lover and that I was his son. They'd been meaning to go away together, but then he was killed in a railway accident. And so she said nothing about it to anyone and for a time believed there was no one else on earth who knew. Then your brother turned up, and he knew everything. This other man, you see —my actual father—had left a little money, which he'd given your brother instructions to look after for her. He came to her and told her about it. But he seemed kind and understanding. She thought she could trust him. And for years he never tried to make any use of his knowledge."

"Years?" Hilda said sharply. "You mean this happened *years* ago?"

"Oh yes."

"And what happened to the money?"

"He gave it to her, little by little. She invented an imaginary rich uncle who sent her presents."

"And what happened next?" Hilda asked.

" Well, it was after you came to live here," Colin said. " I remember that time, though I was away at school. You were all very close friends for a while, weren't you? —then somehow—I don't really know just how—Mother offended your brother. Quite unintentionally she made him furiously angry and he struck back at her at once, threatening to tell my father the whole story."

" And so she decided to tell him herself? "

" It was the only thing for her to do, wasn't it? "

" But neither of them told you? "

The deep lines showed again from his nostrils to his mouth. " No, not then."

" And did it make no difference in your home? "

As he hesitated she saw in a flash of intuition that he wanted desperately to swear that it had made no difference. But he admitted, " Well, I realise now, something went wrong for a while. But I wasn't at home much then and I didn't think much about it. My mother seemed to be ill a good deal—I'm not sure if she really was, or if it was a sort of defence—and my father always seemed to be busy and not to have any time for her or me. And then the curious thing was that he suddenly seemed to want to make an effort to get to know me properly. D'you know what I mean? He stopped treating me like a child and taking me for granted, and started trying to find out what sort of person I really was."

Hilda felt she was beginning to understand how Colin had come by his poise, his cool, hard surface, intended to show no cracks. As she nodded, he hurried on, as if he were glad to be talking.

" That's the only way he ever showed it to me. Or it's the only thing I can remember at the moment. I haven't had long to think about it yet. After Katherine walked out on me yesterday, I brooded on it all for most of the rest of the day. I don't know yet what it really means to me. In the end perhaps it won't mean very much. I hope not. I'm—I'm awfully fond of both my parents."

"And it was your mother who told you, yesterday morning?" Hilda said.

"Yes, she knew I was coming over here to pick Katherine up and spend the day with her and she told me there was something she wanted to tell me first."

"I wonder just what made her do that."

"I suppose she was afraid your brother was going to spring it on me."

"But she didn't tell your father what she was going to do."

"No, not at once."

"It sounds to me," Hilda said, "as if she was afraid that your father's appeal to Stephen and me might work, and so she stuck her oar in first. I mean, I think she must want very badly to smash up your engagement to Katherine."

"But she likes Katherine," he said.

"That might not make any difference." She stood up and crossed to Stephen's desk, looking down at the gaping drawers. "What were you looking for, Colin? Some papers about that sad old story? If there are any, I'm afraid the police must have them by now. But they haven't mentioned them to me, if that's any comfort."

He watched her as she began to collect the papers on the floor and stuff them back into the drawers. She did not try to make any order amongst them. Receipted bills for gas and electricity and for servicing the car, a bulb catalogue, a few unimportant, unpaid bills, one or two personal letters, she thrust them all back as they came. Everything looked to her very innocent and uninteresting.

As she closed the drawers on them, Colin said, "You didn't believe me when I said I wasn't looking for anything."

"Then what were you doing here?" she asked.

"Only indulging a morbid interest in the murder."

At once she noticed the change in his voice. From speaking with a certain openness and warmth, he had returned to the cool, half-mocking tone that he used so often.

"Well, if you don't want to tell me, I suppose I can't make you," she said. "Shall I call Katherine?"

"No." As if Hilda had made a threat of some sort, he started to back towards the window. "I came here to try to see her, but I've changed my mind. There's something I want to think out first. About my mother and what you've been saying about her. All the same, it's the truth that I wasn't really looking for anything. I came here to see Katherine, but when I arrived I suddenly thought I'd like to take a look in here, so I came to the window and found the broken pane and that I could unlatch it quite easily. Cheek on my part, but after all, I'm practically a member of the family, aren't I? Or I was for a little while."

Hilda answered, "Yes, Colin, practically."

"And then I saw the papers on the floor and all the drawers of the desk open, and I wondered who'd been looking for what. And I was taking a look to see what sort of papers in general were kept in the desk, when you came in. It's a thin story, of course, and you won't believe me, but I can't produce a better one."

As he turned and went out, Hilda thought of trying to stop him, of persuading him that he ought to stay and see Katherine, but he went away quickly, hurrying to the gate and letting it slam behind him. A moment later she heard a car start up.

Only then she remembered that what she had come to look for in this room had been a cigarette. She was reaching for the box when, out of the corner of her eye, she saw a car go by.

Ice filled her veins. For an instant she could not move. Then, just as she had done the day before, she plunged out into the garden, ran to the low garden wall, leant over it, and stared down the road after the small grey car that was already almost at the bend of the road. Seeing the stooped silhouette of the driver, she recognised him this time as Colin.

As she turned back into the house, she was shivering. The day before she had not been able to recognise the driver of the small grey car that had driven past the moment after she and Arthur Luckett had discovered the murder. But then her mind had been in a worse state of shock than now. Besides, no one could have been farther from her thoughts at that moment than Colin. To-day she had been prepared, had known, as she ran out into the garden, whom she would see in the car.

Forgetting the cigarette that a little while ago she had wanted so badly, she went to the kitchen, and in a frantic effort to escape for a time from her own thoughts and the responsibility that they seemed to point out to her, she started washing a lettuce and slicing tomatoes.

As she did so, the face of Inspector Crankshaw swam before her, its cheeks long and loose, its eyes little and ironically squinting, and as it had from the first, it seemed like an immense scar on her own conscience, a reminder, like a sharp, recurring pain, of some misdoing of her own.

She would have to tell him, she supposed, about Colin having been the driver of the car. Apart from any other consideration, what was it that Nelson had said? " The driver of that car may be the most important witness in the case." Oh, certainly she would have to tell him.

However, she prepared the cold lunch, called Nelson and Katherine to eat it, pecked at a little of it herself, then left Katherine to do the washing-up, and went upstairs to her room, all without having said anything to anyone about having seen the little grey car again. She had not even mentioned to Nelson or Katherine that she had seen Colin that morning.

It was her intention to rest for a little in peace and quiet, but not to sleep. She wanted to think, to make up her mind what to do with her new knowledge about Colin, about Miss Perriman and her sister, and most of all, about Stephen, her own brother, whom she had known all her life. And that was the hardest part of it, thinking about Stephen. Almost at her first attempt to grapple with the question of what sort of man he had really been, how much maligned by others, how truly evil, the deep, kind oblivion of sleep released her from the effort to find an answer.

When Katherine looked in on her a couple of hours later, to ask her if she would like some tea, Hilda was still asleep on her bed, but, vaguely aware that someone had come into the room, she stirred, shifted the arm that had been crooked under her head and had grown stiff and muttered to herself. As Katherine closed the door softly, Hilda drifted off again into sleep.

It was Nelson who presently woke her, gripping her shoulder, shaking her and shouting at her. She saw his long face hovering above her in the dusk. She had slept a long time, it seemed, and had left something cooking on the stove which had gone dry and was filling all the house now with its unpleasant, acrid odour. In her drowsy state, however, she could not remember what she had been cooking, and was almost inclined to doubt that she had been cooking anything. Potatoes? No. Cabbage? . . .

"Wake up, wake up, Hilda!" Nelson shouted, and suddenly thrusting his hands under her armpits, began to haul her off the bed. "For God's sake, wake up, girl —the house is on fire!"

CHAPTER XI

THERE WAS SMOKE in her bedroom. There was more smoke in the passage. Somewhere in the house there was a roaring sound and everywhere there was the smell of burning.

Hilda staggered to her feet.

" Where's Katherine? "

" I don't know. Out." Nelson gripped Hilda's arm and pulled her towards the door.

" Are you sure? Have you looked in her room? "

Wrenching her arm free, she made for her wardrobe, snatched her fur coat out of it and threw it round her shoulders.

" Yes—come on, come on! " Nelson shouted at her. " It's right below us. We've got to get out of here."

Thrusting her feet into shoes, Hilda ran out into the passage.

" Katherine! " she shouted. " Katherine! "

Nelson had her by the arm again, and was hurrying her to the top of the stairs.

" I told you, she's out," he said.

" Let me make sure."

" For God's sake, Hilda——! "

" It's all right," she said. " It's all right."

One after the other, she opened the doors on the upper landing. The smoke from below, so dense now that both she and Nelson were coughing, billowed into each room. The rooms were all empty. Reassured, she turned to the stairs and plunged down them into the thick yellow cloud that came pouring along the passage. Heat struck her like a blow. The roaring sound was louder, and suddenly through the smoke she saw flames. The floor of the passage was on fire.

But she saw also that as yet she and Nelson were in no danger. Sparks, tossed through the air towards the stairs, were either extinguished or starting a slow smouldering on the carpet where they fell, but the way to the kitchen was still clear of all but the choking smoke.

With Nelson close behind her, Hilda ran out to the kitchen, then straight out into the garden. At first the air seemed sweet and cool and she stood still, breathing it in deeply, but after a moment she realised that even in the garden, it was heavily tainted with the smell of burning, and that the breeze was fanning gust after gust of unnatural heat against her.

Rubbing her smarting eyes and beating at a spark that had settled on her sleeve but had already died, leaving a small charred mark on the fur, she said, " Can't we do anything? Can't we try to stop it? "

" *That* fire? " Nelson said.

" But how did it start? How ever did it get going so quickly? "

He answered grimly, " That's something the police will want to know."

" Did you call the fire-brigade? " she asked.

" The telephone's right in the middle of the blaze," he said. " But I'll go for them now, if you'll promise to stay clear and not try to do anything foolish. Where's the nearest telephone? "

" There's a call-box at the crossroads, opposite Jim Kent's cottage."

" All right, I'll go. But keep clear, d'you understand? Don't try dashing in to save this or that. Do you promise? "

" Yes, yes," she said impatiently, and saw Nelson, a spidery and wild-looking figure in the dusk, go running off round the house.

Following him round to the road, she saw that the fire, without question, had started in Stephen's study.

Seen through the gaping window, the room was a box of flame. And already something was flickering behind the window of her bedroom above. Nelson, who, she supposed, had come in from the river because of the failing light, had not arrived many minutes too soon.

As she stood there alone in the garden, the spectacle of her home on fire absorbed her so deeply that she was curiously unaware of distress. The flames hypnotised her with their ferocity and swift growth. A crashing sound from within the house sent a sharp thrill through her. Filled with an excited sort of dread, which, since there was no fear for her own safety in it, was almost pleasurable, she could have stood watching for hours.

But she was not left alone for long. After a few minutes Nelson came panting back up the road, with Jim Kent and several other men from the cottages. They went into the house by the kitchen door, to see if there was anything that they could do to check the spread of the fire. Then the women and children followed, to gaze, to sympathise, to share in the thrill. Then some passing motorists stopped and soon more people began to arrive from the other end of the village.

Among them were the vicar and his wife and Arthur Luckett. By the time that the fire-brigade arrived from Ledslowe, there was a sizeable crowd to be cleared out of the way before the fire-engines could draw up close to the house.

Watching the helmeted figures as they leapt down, uncoiling the hoses, almost before the men themselves were on the ground, Hilda still felt the excitement that prevented her thinking of what the fire might mean to her. As various people spoke to her, saying what a terrible experience this must be for her, she nodded, wide-eyed, as if she were too upset to speak, yet in some clear corner of her mind, she knew that there was a profound satisfaction in looking on while this thing happened. The fire was wiping out the past about which it had become intolerable to think. The flames were destroying a horror.

"You must come back with us to the vicarage, Hilda—you and Katherine," the vicar's wife said to her.

She and Hilda were good friends. The invitation came naturally and warmly, and it seemed to Hilda that it would be pleasant to accept it, but in the moment before she answered, while her thoughts strayed to Katherine and to where she might be just then, Arthur Luckett interrupted.

"No, they must come to us," he said. "My boy would never forgive me if I allowed them to make any other arrangement."

Distressed, because there was nothing of which she could less have liked the idea than going to stay with the Lucketts, Hilda started to thank him but to refuse his invitation, but she never got beyond the thanks, for in the middle of them he said that that was settled and pushed his way off through the crowd towards the house.

The vicar's wife, with what she obviously thought was tact, said that she had almost forgotten that the Lucketts were practically relations and that of course it would be nicest for Hilda and Katherine to stay with them, instead of in the overcrowded vicarage.

"Trapped," Hilda said to herself, "But for one night only! One night at the very most!"

As she did so, she saw Katherine coming towards her.

They stood side by side in the crowd, watching the fire. At first they seemed to have nothing to say to one another. Hilda wondered if this destruction meant more or less to Katherine than it did to herself. The six years that they had lived here must seem a much longer time in Katherine's life than it did in her own. Katherine, however, was at an age when change came easily, always promising something better than what had been before.

When presently Hilda asked her where she had been that afternoon, Katherine said that she had been to the school where she worked, to explain her absence.

"You can easily go back to-morrow," Hilda said. "There's really nothing to stop you."

"Except that I'm not wanted," Katherine said. "It seems it isn't good for girls to have a murder-suspect amongst them." She was glancing here and there in the crowd, probably looking for Colin, who was not to be seen. Then she once more fixed her gaze steadily on the house. "Why don't they just let it all burn down? It's like trying to save the life of a person with a hopeless disease. No one will ever want to live there again."

"They might save some of our possessions for us," Hilda said.

"How did it start?" Katherine asked.

"I was asleep in my room," Hilda said. "Nelson woke me—that was the first I knew of it."

"Did it start in Father's study?"

"So it seems."

Katherine gave a sharp laugh. "And one doesn't get any insurance when it's arson, does one?"

Hilda cast a quick look round her. "If you'd lower your voice when you say that sort of thing, it wouldn't do any harm."

Katherine put an arm round her shoulders. "I'm sorry. But d'you know, I thought you'd ask me indignantly how I could have such a wicked idea. And I almost wish you had. I don't want you to start getting mean and suspicious like the rest of us. Who do you think started it? Miss Perriman?"

"How could she have done it?"

"Well, she was over here this morning, wasn't she? You know, when I brought her in to see you, I'd just found her snooping in at the window. She tried to laugh it off in a horsey sort of way, saying she'd always suffered from morbid curiosity.... Why, what's the matter?"

For Hilda's shoulders, encircled by Katherine's arm, had just given a violent jerk.

Hilda was remembering how Colin had used that same excuse to explain his presence in Stephen's room.

" I suppose lots of people suffer from morbid curiosity," she said. " But do you think—do you think a person could leave something behind in a room that could go on fire some hours later? "

" Couldn't they? "

" I don't know."

" A small time-bomb of some sort," Katherine suggested with a certain zest.

" It isn't a joke," Hilda said desolately. " And why should—anyone—have done it? "

" Well, suppose Miss Perriman thought Father had had some sort of evidence against her sister, something in writing. And suppose she had a try last night at finding it, but realised, after she'd been interrupted by you and then frightened off by Jim Kent, that she didn't stand a chance of laying her hands on it. She might have decided the only way to destroy it was to destroy the whole house too."

Hilda said nothing.

Realising that her suggestion had upset her, Katherine let her arm drop from Hilda's shoulders.

" Well, I think I'd better see about getting us a room for the night somewhere," she said. " I'll ring up the Dragon in Ledslowe, shall I? "

" No," Hilda said, " we're going to the Lucketts."

" No! "

" Yes," Hilda said, clearly and firmly. For she had to see Colin again. She had to come to some decision about him. " Arthur very kindly invited us both, and I accepted."

In Katherine's eyes there was a blaze of anger. Without another word, she walked away.

Hilda saw her go to Nelson, who had just appeared from behind the house. His face was reddened by heat and excitement and patterned with zebra-like streaks of sweat and soot. He bent his head so that Katherine could speak into his ear, ran a grimy hand over his bald head, looked uncertain, tugged at his lower lip, then answered her. Hilda did not know what he said, but later, when Arthur Luckett, as grimy as Nelson, came to drive them to his home, Katherine went without protest.

The Lucketts' house was at the far end of the village. It was a long time since Hilda had been there, a long time since she had even seen the house. It stood far back from the road, screened by a high yew hedge and a belt of chestnuts, so that to a passer-by only the twisted chimneys were visible. It was a big house, but a homely rather than a grand one, built of rosy brick and ivy-grown, and still a farmhouse, with barns and cowsheds near it.

Valerie Luckett and Colin came to the door together when the car stopped there.

Valerie was about the same height as her son, was very slender and quick and restless in her movements. Her brown hair, in which the light from behind her lit glints of copper, was cut short and brushed back in soft feathery little curls from her oval face. Her blue eyes, which were so like Colin's, were remarkably bright. There was always a great deal of animation in her face, and of emphasis in her high, sweet voice, yet neither was really expressive.

Meeting Hilda on the steps of the house, she held out her hands and clasped both of Hilda's. She said all the things that might have been expected of her in the way of concern and welcome. Talking fast, and leaving no time for any answer, she gave Katherine a swift kiss, sent her husband away to have a wash, told Colin to take drinks into the drawing-room, took Hilda and Katherine upstairs to the rooms that were being prepared for them, drew the curtains, switched on the electric fire in each room, offered the use of her own clothes and cosmetics, and only then, suddenly, standing by the door of Hilda's bedroom, looked at her in silence, meeting her eyes with a long, glittering, unrevealing stare.

It was a silence of only a moment. Almost instantly Valerie was talking again, telling Hilda to come down for a drink as soon as she was ready, or, if she preferred, to stay here and rest. Nothing could have been kinder and friendlier. Yet as the sound of Valerie's quick footsteps died away down the stairs, Hilda, left alone in the big, pleasant room with its beamed ceiling and fourposter-bed, felt that there had been nothing but silence since she had come into the house, a singularly chill, embarrassing silence.

It was the same presently, when, washed and changed, she went down to the drawing-room. Valerie was asking Arthur all about the fire. She asked her questions eagerly and gaily, and interrupted him to tell a story of a fire that she had been in when she had been a girl, a fire caused by a couple of tea-cloths, hung up to dry, falling on to a lighted gas-ring and making such an astonishing amount of smoke that a nervous neighbour, seeing it eddy out of the kitchen window, telephoned for the fire-brigade.

" It was London, of course," Valerie said, " and within minutes—I mean, *minutes*—the whole street was filled with fire-engines, and firemen were racing into the house with their hoses, demanding a fire to put out. And there was my mother, sheepishly sweeping up the remains of the burnt tea-cloths."

The story ended with a rippling laugh, and was followed by another. But to Hilda the feeling of silence around her persisted. At first this was bewildering, but presently she realised that although words were pouring out, not only from Valerie but a few from Hilda herself, from Arthur and from Katherine, they could at no point be added up to mean the same as was in the mind of the speaker. So it was almost the same as if nothing were being said.

Colin alone was actually silent. He offered no explanation of why he had not come with Arthur Luckett to help at the fire. He did not try to talk to Katherine. Looking incredibly like his mother, or rather, as she might have looked if her nervous, restless features had been carved in stone, he sat with his eyes on her, perhaps listening to her intently, perhaps not listening at all. Hilda thought that if he had sat looking at her like that she would have felt very afraid of him.

The moment that that thought had crossed her mind, it came to her that frightened was what Valerie was. She could not look at Colin. She could talk on and on to everyone else but never to him. She could make a desperate pretence of unawareness of his strange concentration on her. Yet she could not withdraw her attention from him for a second. Her son's silence possessed her and terrified her.

To a lesser extent it seemed to have affected Arthur. There was embarrassment on his heavy, ruddy face, and at times the signs of a determined effort not to reveal much of what he was feeling. As soon as dinner was over, without waiting for coffee, he muttered something about work and went out. But before he went he laid one of his big and violent-looking hands on Katherine's shoulder in a gentle gesture of reassurance.

Katherine started and looked as if she were about to burst into tears. Colin did not appear to have noticed.

As soon as she could, Hilda went upstairs to bed. She fiercely regretted the impulse that had made her insist on Katherine's coming to the Lucketts. For what good could it do her to see Colin in his present mood? It would have been far more sensible of her to have gone to Inspector Crankshaw instead and told him about her discovery of Colin in Stephen's room.

Meanwhile, she wondered, did anyone besides herself know of his visit? Had anyone else seen him come and go?

There was a knock at her door.

Supposing that it was Katherine, she called, " Come in."

The door opened and Valerie entered.

She closed the door behind her and leant against it. She seemed exhausted, with all the vitality drained out of her slender, brittle-looking body. Her blue eyes looked very large in her pale face. Hilda was taken by surprise by a strong impulse of sympathy for her. Would Valerie have grown into this tense and rather unreal person if the man whom she had loved better than she had loved Arthur Luckett had not been killed in a railway accident? Hilda had often asked herself a similar question when certain of her own qualities had struck her as unsatisfactory, so why should she not allow Valerie the benefit of a certain doubt?

Valerie was gazing at her.

" Well, Hilda? Well? " she said quietly.

Hilda, sitting at the dressing-table, brushing her hair, and noticing that the smell of the fire was clinging to it, as well as to her clothes, echoed her uncertainly, " Well? "

" Did he do it? "

" Did—he——? " The words came limping.

" Did my son murder your brother? Did he? "

Carefully Hilda laid the hairbrush down, the hairbrush that Valerie had lent her.

" Is that what you believe, Valerie? "

" I'm asking you what you believe. He had a reason to do it."

" The reason you gave him," Hilda said. " Why did you do that? "

" If I hadn't decided to tell him the truth, he'd have heard it sooner or later from Stephen. That would have been a far worse shock."

"But Stephen had had plenty of time to tell him, if he'd wanted to."

"Perhaps the right moment hadn't come yet, the moment when he could inflict the most pain."

The words tore the fragile defences that Hilda had been building around her affection for Stephen. The fact that he had not used his knowledge of Colin and his family in any attempt to spoil Katherine's happiness seemed, for the time being, her most precious memory of him. But Valerie's bitter suggestion made it appear a feeble prop for faith.

"So that's why you did it—to save Colin pain?" Hilda said coldly.

"Do you think I did it because I hoped he would go and murder Stephen?" Valerie asked.

"No, I was thinking about Katherine—Katherine and Colin."

"I know what you're thinking," Valerie said. "The possessive mother, wrecking her son's chance of happiness to save some for herself. It's easier for you to attack me with that than to defend Stephen."

"I haven't been trying to defend Stephen," Hilda said. "Perhaps he was a very bad man, and I was just too close to him to notice it. He wasn't bad to me, but I suppose nobody's bad to everyone."

"He'd have ruined my life if I'd let him," Valerie said. "Cold-bloodedly ruined it."

"Yet he wasn't at all cold-blooded. He was revengeful, he was moody and suspicious and he always thougth people wanted to harm him. He was hurt much too easily and always thought it had been done on purpose. He was bitter and intolerant and awfully hard to get along with "—she gave a deep sigh—" but not cold-blooded."

Valerie laughed.

"I'm sorry for you, Hilda. I know what it can be like, looking for crumbs of comfort. That's what I've been doing all day. If my son's suspected of killing your brother, then it'll be my fault, because I'm a possessive mother. You see, I'm admitting it. I didn't have to say anything. Arthur didn't want me to say anything. He thought he could appeal to Stephen's better nature, through you. But I didn't give him time to try how his plan would work out, I told Colin the whole truth myself. And in the evening Stephen—died."

Some of Valerie's vitality had returned while she was speaking. She let go of the door and came a few steps forward. Standing tense and erect in the middle of the room, she said, " And you may have noticed, Colin isn't speaking to me much to-day. I was prepared for that, of course. I know him. I know that when he gets a shock, the only thing he can think of is that he mustn't show it. All his strength goes into that. He's very unsure of himself, but dreads the thought that anyone should ever find it out. I knew he'd go silent and unapproachable for days, but I thought that would be all —except that I sort of hoped there'd be an end of the engagement. I don't mean that I don't like Katherine, or that I wish her any harm. It was just the thought of being linked for ever to Stephen. It didn't seem tolerable. I thought something drastic *had* to be done. But if I'd thought, if I'd ever dreamt, that this other shock was coming, I'd—well, I'd have murdered Stephen myself rather than do what I did. I've been in hell all day, Hilda—truly in hell."

Hilda picked up the hairbrush and turning to the mirror, gave her hair a few deliberate strokes.

" Do you know where Colin says he was at the time of the murder? " she asked.

" Out driving somewhere," Valerie answered. " He's got a new car. Why? "

Carefully unemphatic, Hilda answered, " Because I think he was somewhere near our house. Ask Arthur about it. I think he saw Colin drive past the window only a moment after we'd found Stephen. And if it was Colin, he must have seen Arthur, yet he drove on fast, he didn't stop."

"Oh, God!" Valerie said softly.

"I may be wrong. Ask Arthur about it," Hilda said. "He can tell you. I only spoke of it because it seemed to me you wanted to know the worst."

"That's what one thinks, that one's strong enough to know the worst," Valerie said, "when all one really wants is to be told one's fears are ridiculous. I'm not strong at all. I'm not at all brave. Do you know what I did when I heard about the fire? I fainted. I knew Colin had been over to try to see Katherine this afternoon, so I fainted."

"So you knew he'd been over to us?"

"He'd told me he was going," Valerie said. "But he didn't say anything about it when he came back."

"And it was because you fainted that he didn't come with Arthur to help?"

"Of course. He couldn't—I wouldn't let him—leave me."

"But why should he have wanted to set our house on fire?" Hilda asked. "Why should anyone, if it comes to that? That's what I simply can't understand. If it was to destroy evidence, it was much too late. The police spent hours last night examining and photographing everything and going through Stephen's papers. If there was ever anything dangerous to any of you, it had been taken away already. And Colin isn't stupid or ignorant. He'd have known that."

"So you don't actually believe he had anything to do with the fire?" Valerie said eagerly. "Or with the murder? I'm hysterical, I'm stupid—that's what everyone tells me. That's all it is, isn't it? Nobody's actually going to think he had anything to do with either."

"I don't know," Hilda said. "I don't know any more than you do. Perhaps not as much."

The eagerness dropped out of Valerie's tone. " I don't know anything. Probably I'm only so worried because of my own guilty conscience. That's something I've had to live with, for one reason or another, an awful lot of my life—that and an awful lot of forgiveness—and perhaps that hasn't been good for me. You know, Stephen's the only person who ever really tried to call me to account. I suppose that's why I hated him so, rather than for what he threatened me with. That didn't matter. He didn't realise it, but Arthur was always so fond of Colin that he'd never have divorced me, and so I always knew I was quite safe. And I expect that makes you think I'm not a very nice person." She turned to the door. " I always think most of myself, don't I? People tell you that's a good recipe for unhappiness. Good night, Hilda."

" Good night, Valerie."

It was only after Valerie had gone, that it occurred to Hilda to wonder where Valerie herself had been at the time of Stephen's murder.

But if all that Valerie had just been saying was true, then she, of all people, had had no motive for the murder. She had freed herself from Stephen's power by telling her secret herself to the only two people to whom it seemed to be of any importance. Really, of the three Lucketts, only Colin, suffering, as he had been that day, from a great emotional shock, might conceivably have worked himself into a state in which it had seemed necessary to kill.

But perhaps Valerie had not been telling the truth. Perhaps the three Lucketts had joined together in concocting a story which would keep Valerie, if not her son, safe from the danger of being suspected of Stephen's murder.

Getting into bed, Hilda seemed to hear the voice of Inspector Crankshaw speaking in her ear. " Everyone has secrets, Miss Gazeley. I have. You have. . . ."

Hilda switched off the bedside-lamp and settled herself comfortably, but she did not close her eyes. The darkness of the room was pleasant to them. It soothed the scratchy feeling of tiredness that they had had all day, and that had been made far worse by the smoke. But her brain still felt too active for sleep, and projected curious images on to the darkness before her.

Side by side she saw two different pictures of Colin. One the picture that she herself had had of him, at least until the conversation that she had had with him that morning, the other the one that had just been given to her by his mother. Hilda had always thought him very clear in his mind about his own feelings and opinions, and more than a little indifferent to those things in other people. Valerie had said that he was very unsure of himself, and very frightened of having that fact discovered. Which was the truth?

That was Colin's secret.

"Everyone has secrets, Miss Gazeley. I have. You have. He has . . . *Nous avons, Vous avez, Ils ont.* . . ."

She was not aware of the point at which her eyes closed, or the time when she and the images that peopled the disturbed darkness around her seemed to enter into a different and more active relationship, yet there she was presently, back in the schoolroom, trying to memorise French verbs and being told that she was stupid, stupid, stupid, and more than that, had left one of them out.

And that was not merely stupid, it was wrong. One must not keep a French verb to oneself. If one commits such an enormity, said her governess, bringing close to her a face with long, loose cheeks and little, sharp, raffish eyes, which had looked on all the evil of the world, she must expect to have these terrible feelings of guilt. Try again. *J'ai, tu as* . . . No, no, we've had that one. Try again, try again. It's *your* secret we want, Miss Gazeley. . . .

CHAPTER XII

KATHERINE, COMING IN and drawing back the curtains to show the grey square of the window, woke Hilda at eight o'clock. She felt sick and shivery, as if she had woken with 'flu.

Katherine was wearing a man's camel-hair dressing-gown, much too wide for her at the shoulders, over a nightgown that was several inches too long. The one, Hilda supposed, belonged to Colin, the other to Valerie. With her rumpled hair and with her bare toes showing under the nightgown, they made Katherine look about half her age. Yet her expression was not childish. There was a haunted preoccupation in it, with a pallor and a weariness which suggested that she had slept less well than Hilda.

"We aren't staying here to-day, are we?" she asked. "I don't think we ought to."

"No," Hilda said. "We'll go to a hotel in Ledslowe, unless we can camp out at home."

"There's nothing much left to camp in," Katherine told her.

"How do you know?"

"Colin and I went to take a look last night, after you'd gone to bed."

"So you're speaking to one another again, are you?" Hilda said. "In that case, why are you so anxious to move out?"

"Because speaking," Katherine said, "is just about all we're doing."

"And which of you is it that wants it like that?"

Katherine shrugged the slim shoulders that were covered by the enveloping dressing-gown. "Both, I expect. It seems simplest for the time being."

"Aren't you in love with him any more?"

Katherine gave Hilda the derisive look that she knew so well.

"You say that as if being in love were like—like being in a hot bath or out of it. Something you know quite for certain."

"And isn't it?"

The mockery deeped in Katherine's grey eyes. Then suddenly they swam with tears. Clutching the dressing-gown about her, she turned away.

She turned towards the dressing-table, and when she spoke again, it was as if she were picking up some old argument with her own reflection in the looking-glass.

"I don't know—perhaps it is. Yes, it is, I think. But we won't stay here, will we? You won't let them persuade you?"

"Perhaps they won't try to," Hilda said.

"Oh, they will. Mr. Luckett will. He wants a chance to be nice to us."

"In that case, why not stay?"

"Because of the things they all think about Father."

"But suppose—just suppose those things are true?"

"All the more reason for leaving!"

Hilda shook her head. "That sounds more like pride than anything else."

"Well, pride's a good thing to have."

"Not always. No, certainly not always. Not if——" Hilda had been about to say that pride was not necessarily a good thing to have if one were in love, but found herself unwilling to repeat the phrase so soon, to hammer on it with sentimental insistence. "Not if one's in the wrong," she said lamely.

"Believe it or not, that's something I've heard about," Katherine said, with a dry laugh. "Only when I'm hurt, I like to hit back. That's rather like Father, isn't it? Except that sometimes I can manage to apologise afterwards, which I don't think he ever did. But it doesn't always help. One can go too far, it seems. One can say things that can't be taken back."

"What did you say to Colin that you can't take back?"

"Just certain things about his lack of courage. So let's not stay here to-day. Promise me we won't stay here."

"All right, we won't," Hilda said, trying to sound decisive and strong-minded, but at the same time hoping that Arthur Luckett would not feel too deeply the desire to be nice to her and Katherine, because she did not really feel fit to argue with him, or with anyone.

When presently she went downstairs, she found him waiting for her in the dining-room. He had had his own breakfast and was striding restlessly about the room, fiercely smoking a mangled cigarette. Like his clothes, his cigarettes always looked as if they suffered unnecessary violence at his hands, but his look, as he greeted Hilda, was mild and worried.

Pouring out coffee for her, he said, " Valerie got up some time ago and went out for a walk. She had a bad night, poor girl, and when that happens, she generally gets up and goes out. She doesn't sleep too well at the best of times, and with worries like she's got on her mind at the moment, it was only to be expected. How did you sleep? Not too well, I suppose. But I hope you were comfortable."

"I slept surprisingly well," Hilda answered, "and I was very comfortable."

"Good," he said, bringing her bacon and eggs from the sideboard. "I'm glad to hear it. And I'm very glad you're here, Hilda. I'm glad you agreed to come. For our sakes, Valerie's and mine, as well as Colin's. We made some mistakes in the past that we want to put right. It's generous of you to let us try."

Hilda thought that Valerie's effort the evening before to correct any mistake that she might have made had not been very great, but she answered, " I don't know what mistakes you mean, Arthur."

" Our thinking that you could have known anything whatever about what Stephen tried to do to us." He stepped back to the hearthrug and stood warming himself there, close to the wood fire that crackled on the open hearth. " I know you know about it now. Colin told us you'd heard it all from Katherine. The silly young fool threw it all up at her as soon as he heard it from Valerie. My fault, that, really, most of it. I ought to have seen long ago that he'd have to know the facts. As it was, hearing it suddenly like that from Valerie, who tends to dramatise things at the best of times, he got a quite exaggerated idea of what had happened? "

" Did he, Arthur? "

He pretended not to notice the scepticism in her question.

" Yes, he . . . That is, well . . . Confound it, Hilda, you know what Valerie's like! Look at the things she said to you last night. She told me about it. Pretending she was afraid Colin might be suspected of the murder of your brother. Good God, think of it! "

" But you were afraid of that yourself, weren't you? Or why did you try to stop me seeing Colin driving by in his new car? "

He brought his big hands together, cracking the knuckles with almost the sound of a shot being fired.

" Because that took some explaining, didn't it? He saw me and he didn't stop. How would you have explained that yourself, if I'd let you see him a split second after we'd discovered Stephen. But it's true I was badly worried when I saw him. I didn't know anything then about what Valerie'd told him that morning, so I thought there couldn't be any reason on earth for him not to stop when he saw me, unless he knew something about the murder."

" But, Arthur, it was only if Valerie or someone had

told him that that he could have had the faintest motive for murdering Stephen."

" I didn't say murdering him, I said knowing something about it."

" Yes, but still . . ."

" No! " he said, his hands making that fearful cracking sound again as they fought with each other. " No, Hilda! I did not suspect him of the murder. I know the boy. I've taken some trouble to get to know him. I wanted to find out what kind of person it was I'd sheltered and—and cared for. I dare say I know him better than I would if he were my own son. The fact that he's so different from me, got completely different interests and all—that's a thing I dare say it's always a bit hard for a man not to resent in a son—well, I stopped struggling against it. I started to take him as he was. I got to understand him. And so I never thought for a moment he'd done the murder, when I saw him drive past your house. I just thought—well, damn it, I don't know what I thought, but I didn't think it'd do any harm if you didn't see him."

" And do you know now why he drove straight on? "

" Of course I do! " He started to walk up and down in front of the fireplace, taking two or three long strides in each direction, catching his feet in the edges of the rug and soon bringing it to as rumpled a condition as the collar and tie that he had put on only that morning. " Once I knew what Valerie'd done, there wasn't any question. He didn't want to see me, that was all. He'd come there to see Katherine and try to put things right after the trouble they'd had with each other in the morning, and there he saw me standing at the french window. And he wasn't ready to face me yet, after what he'd found out that morning. Colin takes his time to make up his mind what he thinks about a thing, and a thing like that . . . Well, you can see he doesn't know yet where he stands. But he'll sort it out on his own and then we'll get straight. It's all right, I'm not worrying."

His voice was hoarse with worry. At first Hilda took it for the natural worry of an uncomplicated and warm-hearted man who has given his heart to someone far more complex than himself, and who, therefore, in a crisis, finds himself with nothing but an uncertain faith to help him understand what may be happening in the heart of the other. To Arthur, Colin's feelings, however strong, would always be hedged around with all kinds of incomprehensible and disturbing subtleties.

But as Hilda gave up the not very successful attempt to eat the bacon and eggs that Arthur had given her, and drank some coffee, a different explanation of his worry suggested itself. Suppose it had really very little to do with Colin, but only with what Colin had seen while he was driving by.

Nelson had called the driver of the car the most important witness in the case.

She stood up. She went to one of the tall windows and stood looking out at the garden. She wanted to ask Arthur where Valerie had been at the time of the murder. But even with her back to him, she could not bring out the words.

" It looks like rain," she said.

" I don't think so," Arthur said. " Not to-day."

" About Katherine and Colin . . ."

" Ah," he said, " I meant to say something about that. I meant to say, give them time, it'll be all right."

" Valerie doesn't want it to be all right, does she? "

" She does really," he said. " You mustn't take too much notice of the things she says. And she likes Katherine very much, you know. She's often said so."

" Perhaps she does, but still . . ."

Again she tried to make herself ask that question as to Valerie's whereabouts at the time when Stephen was killed. But how could you ask a question like that of a man like Arthur Luckett, an honest, generous man, who had already had, so she thought, rather more than his share of trouble?

"Listen, Hilda, don't worry about that," he said, and came to stand beside her, as he had been standing when together they had heard the crash and the cry from Stephen's room. "I'm going to talk to the boy this morning. I'm not going to say much, but I'm just going to remind him that his mother's got a—well, a certain way with her. He knows all about it. He's not as much under her thumb as you think—or as she thinks. It's just the shock he's had that's sort of paralysed him for the moment, and he's got the feeling that Katherine's turned against him, because of what he told her about her father. Well, all that was true, you know, but that doesn't make it any easier for her—I can see that. So they've both just got to have time. But I'll talk to him."

She turned and looked at him. "It *was* true? Stephen tried to blackmail Valerie?"

"It wasn't exactly blackmail," he said. "He didn't ask for money. He just wanted her in his power. He wanted her to be afraid of him." He put a hand on her shoulder. "But listen, Hilda, we must forget about all that. We must be friends. Don't you think we can be?"

She moved away from him. She liked him probably as much as she had ever liked anybody, and wanted to be friends with him, but after what he had just said, she wanted only to run away and hide her head.

"We must go and take a look at the house this morning, Katherine and I," she said. "It'll be a mess, a horrible mess, but we'd better face it."

He was looking after her with a puzzled and hurt expression as she went out in search of Katherine. She had had her breakfast earlier and was waiting impatiently for Hilda in her bedroom. Hilda put on her fur coat, thankful that she had had the presence of mind to save it, and they started out together.

As they left the Lucketts' house, Katherine asked, "Did you tell them we aren't staying on?"

"No," Hilda said, "I forgot all about it."

Katherine exclaimed in annoyance.

"Besides," Hilda said, "I'm not sure now we shouldn't stay."

"Ah, I see, you didn't forget, you decided. Well, I'm not staying on," Katherine said. "Mrs. Luckett doesn't really want us to. It's just that she's afraid Colin may be angry if they don't try to make us."

"Well, I've been talking to Arthur," Hilda began, but Katherine, looking offended, had hurried on ahead, walking too fast for Hilda to keep up with her.

As they passed the church and went through the turnstile on to the path through the wood, it seemed to Hilda that the smell of burning still hung on the air beneath the trees, mingled with the dank smell of rotting leaves. Approaching the house, the stale smell of the fire grew stronger. Yet at first sight, from the gate into the kitchen garden, the building showed no signs of damage, and Hilda was aware of sharp disappointment. Following Katherine towards it, she realised that she would have felt great satisfaction in finding it razed to the ground.

But at least, as she was able to decide when she saw the front of the house, it was hardly habitable. The end that had contained Stephen's study, with her bedroom above it, had been quite destroyed. Though the outer walls were still standing, the roof and the floors had fallen in, and except for scattered piles of slate and a few thick, blackened beams, had disappeared into a slime of sodden ash.

Picking his way cautiously amongst the debris, and looking at a distance rather like an archæologist, quietly at work in the ruins of some long deserted temple, was Inspector Crankshaw.

Hearing Katherine and Hilda in the garden, he came

towards them, ducking under a beam and stepping out on to the lawn through the gap that had once been the french window.

He said good morning to them. He said a number of sympathetic things about the loss of their home. He looked as if he would have liked to pat each of them kindly on the head, and was restrained from doing so only by the fact that his hands were extremely dirty.

Then, without any change in his benevolent manner, and sounding as if he knew that what he had to tell them would give them pleasure, he remarked, " By the way, we've found the weapon that killed Mr. Gazeley. We found it in the river. Isn't that interesting? "

His cheerfulness struck Hilda dumb. She would have liked to walk away quickly before he could start to describe, in that friendly tone, the implement that had been used to split Stephen's skull.

Katherine also seemed at a loss, but she managed to ask, " What's interesting—the weapon or where you found it? "

" Mainly where we found it," Crankshaw said. " The weapon itself is a garden hoe—the short-handled kind, very heavy. I've questioned your gardener. He says it came from your tool-shed."

" We have one like that—yes," Hilda said, speaking quickly because she wanted to prevent too clear an image of the hoe forming in her mind, yet immediately seeing with fearful distinctness a picture of the short, stout handle and the heavily weighted metal head. " But are you sure it's the same one? I mean, who would have known where to find it, except just ourselves? "

" Well, of course, there's Kent himself," Crankshaw said. " And almost anyone, wanting something heavy to do a murder with, might think of looking in a tool-shed."

" And that means," Katherine said, " that whoever

went into my father's study, taking that hoe, went there to do murder."

"That's right," Crankshaw said, nodding his big head, like a schoolmaster pleased with a bright pupil. "You wouldn't just happen to have a thing like that along with you when you paid a visit, would you? So the murder was premeditated. It wasn't a case of a quarrel flaring up unexpectedly and someone hitting out harder than he meant to. No. Someone went to the tool-shed, looking for a weapon, someone who thought that Miss Gazeley would be at church, and who knew where to find Mr. Gazeley. Someone, that's to say, who knew quite a bit about your habits."

"That could be lots of people," Katherine said.

"Yes, unfortunately. It could be Kent, who says he was digging in his own garden at the time of the murder, and who happened to come in here late the same night and find Miss Gazeley unconscious in the study. It could be young Mr. Luckett, who says he was out in his new car, but says he was in such a state of mind because of a quarrel he'd had with you that morning that he can't remember just where he went. It couldn't be his father, because he was sitting here in the garden with Miss Gazeley, but it could be Mrs. Luckett, who says she was lying down in her room, but who can't produce anyone else to say so too, because, being Sunday, both the servants were out. It could be Mr. Wingard, who says he was walking up through the wood and who saw Miss Gazeley and Mr. Luckett sitting talking on the garden bench, but who didn't see one or two other things he really ought to have seen, so perhaps wasn't really where he said he was at all. It could be Miss Perriman, who says she was working in her garden, but it couldn't be Mrs. Frearson, because she was having an evening out with Stan Brown." He paused and from his great height looked down with sinister benignity at Katherine. "And it could be you, even if you're a little small for the part.

It's a heavy hoe, as I said, very heavy. But you're quite a strong young woman, aren't you? Played hockey at school, perhaps. Athletic."

From his tone, it might all have been meant as a joke.

With a pinched look about her lips, Katherine said, " You said it was *where* you found the hoe that's interesting."

" That's right," he said, " it was in the river, just about opposite the far end of the house, where anyone coming out of the back door could have thrown it. Yet if that's what he did—he or she—why didn't Mr. Wingard see it happen? He was standing where he could see right along the river bank behind the house, yet he didn't see anyone rush across the lawn and dump that hoe in the water. Well, isn't that interesting? "

" Couldn't it have been thrown into the water from the house? " Katherine suggested.

" I'm not saying it absolutely couldn't have," Crankshaw said. " The murderer could have stood in the scullery inside the back door, out of sight of Mr. Wingard. He could have gripped the hoe with both hands, spun it round his head a few times to get up velocity and let go of it so that it flew out of the door and fell in the river. By a miracle—but you understand, it would have taken a genuine, dyed-in-the-wool miracle—he might somehow not have smashed up every single thing in the scullery. But he could not have made the hoe fall in the water without a very big splash, and Mr. Wingard would have seen that splash."

" All right," Katherine said, her cheeks turning pink, " it was a stupid suggestion. But what did happen, then? "

Crankshaw shook his head. " Oh no, it wasn't a stupid suggestion. It's an idea I've considered very carefully. You have to consider everything, even the things that seem absurd at first sight, because it's only when you've done that that you've the right to say to someone that what he's telling you couldn't be the truth. *Couldn't* be, you understand. Not merely mightn't be, not merely doesn't sound too plausible, but *couldn't* be."

Hilda had noticed that during the last sentence the good nature had faded from his voice. She was glad of it. To hear its grimness was in its way as much of a relief as it might have been suddenly to see in her path rocks that she had known well were there somewhere before her, but which had been concealed in deep fog.

"So you believe Mr. Wingard's lying about what he saw," she said.

"Well, look at it this way," he said. "The murder happened when you and Mr. Luckett were sitting in the garden. You ran to the window here. It was bolted inside and the curtains were drawn. You ran round the house to the back door. You went to the study. You found the curtains drawn back and the window wide open. You thought the murderer had run out that way as soon as you were out of sight round the corner of the house. You ran out yourselves, but all you saw was a small grey car going past. Now the murderer may have been in that car, or the driver may have seen the murderer come out and run away through the kitchen garden into the wood. I think if the murderer did leave the house that way, it has to be one or the other. And if he kept close to the front wall of the house, Mr. Wingard wouldn't have seen him, so there's no need to doubt that possibility on that account. But all the same, how did the hoe get into the river?"

He waited, giving them a chance to make further helpful suggestions.

When neither of them spoke, he went on, "You might say, of course, that the murderer brought it back later, under cover of darkness, and put it in the river opposite the back door here just on purpose to confuse us. Well, he could have done. It's one of those stupid-sounding ideas that one musn't absolutely rule out. But I think it's easier to believe that he didn't get out by the french window at all. I think he threw the windows open just to make you and Mr. Luckett think he'd gone that way and waste a few minutes looking up and down the road, while actually, after having hidden in a cupboard or just behind a door, he slipped out by the back door, dumped the hoe in the river and made off. But that means, either that Mr. Wingard saw him, or else that Mr. Wingard wasn't standing where he said he was at the time of the murder. In either case, he hasn't told the whole truth."

"But I've talked to him about that," Hilda said, "and he explained it. He was watching Mr. Luckett and me. He saw us rush round the corner of the house, and then rush out at the front. He watched us while we were watching the car go by, and he watched the car too. And it must have been just about then that the murderer slipped out by the back door. Isn't that so? And he could hardly have been watching everything."

"It could be," Crankshaw said. "On the other hand, it could be that Mr. Wingard simply wasn't there at all, or else that he saw someone come out of the house, and go down to the river, whom for some reason he wants to protect. People do that sort of thing sometimes. Even lawyers, who ought to know better. Very trying of them, but it's important to remember they sometimes do it. And that brings me to the fire last night. Someone set that fire. It couldn't have got going as fast as it did if there hadn't been petrol to help it. And the most likely reason for it seems to be that the murderer, or someone trying to help the murderer, wanted to obliterate something in that room. Something we missed, or something he thinks we may have missed. Can't you suggest what that could possibly have been?"

Hilda shook her head. So did Katherine.

"But I can tell you something more about Mr. Wingard," Hilda said, "which proves that he was standing where he said. He told me he saw Mr. Luckett standing beside me with his hand on my shoulder, and that's just how he *was* standing when we heard my brother cry out, and to have seen that, Mr. Wingard must have been where he said he was, or somewhere near it."

For a moment she thought that Crankshaw had not been listening to her. He was looking at her, but absently, and he had started tugging at his lower lip. He looked as if his thoughts had suddenly gone wandering off in some quite new direction, and it was only with an effort that he was able to bring them back to what she had said.

Still tugging at his lip, he muttered, " Ah, so Mr. Luckett was standing beside you. . . . Very interesting. . . . Yes, certainly. However, I must add to that that I still don't believe for a moment in your explanation of why Mr. Wingard didn't see the murderer come out at the back of the house and go down to the river." The grimness had suddenly come back into his voice. The fog of affability had swirled away, leaving bare once more the dangerous, sharp rocks of his personality. " Now please excuse me."

As if it had been Hilda and Katherine who had been delaying him, keeping him from getting ahead with more important matters, he turned and disappeared round the corner of the house.

As she watched him go, Katherine said uneasily, " Now I wonder what he meant by that."

" Well, he seems to believe that Nelson's protecting the murderer," Hilda said.

" Then he doesn't know Nelson. I don't really see him taking risks for somebody else, do you? And who is there here whom he knows well enough to want to protect? "

" You and me, possibly."

" But we don't need protecting." Katherine slipped her arm through Hilda's. " Now let's go in and see if we can possibly sleep here to-night."

Reluctantly, because she did not want to go into the house at all, Hilda let herself be drawn towards the door.
" But, Katherine—— "
" Well? "
Hilda had been about to comment on Crankshaw's moment of absentmindedness, just before his abrupt departure. She had a feeling that that, in the whole interview, was the moment that counted, and she wanted to know if Katherine had felt the same thing. Trying to recall what each of them had been saying just before that swift alteration in his manner, Hilda remembered that she had just told him how she and Arthur Luckett had been standing side by side when they heard Stephen cry out. But Crankshaw had not seemed to listen to her after the first few words. So perhaps it had been something to do with what he himself had been saying before it, something about fire. . . .
But before she managed to say any of this to Katherine, they had reached the door and Katherine had pushed it open, and there, face to face with them across the narrow hall, standing motionless in the kitchen doorway, was Mrs. Frearson.

CHAPTER XIII

STANDING THERE, white-faced and still in the small, ash-strewn hall, she might have been taken for a waxwork. So Hilda thought, then at once wished intensely that it had been Mrs. Frearson's resemblance to a marble statue or to a figure in Dresden china that had occurred to her. The smooth, delicate pallor of her skin, so colourless that the faint blue veins on her temples were noticeable, might have made one think of marble. Her wide, grey-blue eyes, which were curiously shiny without looking alive, and the cold, subtle curve of her lips, might have made one think of painted china. And neither of these thoughts would have started up in Hilda's mind recollections of the expressionless, waxen features of convicted murderesses, seen long ago, on a visit that she had once made with Stephen to the Chamber of Horrors.

"Good morning," she said, feeling that if that conventional greeting, in the circumstances, seemed rather ridiculous, nothing else would really have been any better.

Mrs. Frearson herself seemed disinclined to say anything at all. She merely looked at Hilda, then over her shoulder at the door.

Hilda quickly drew it shut behind her. For that look might mean that Mrs. Frearson was contemplating making a run for it, and since Hilda had never before really seen her face to face, never yet heard her speak, this was an opportunity not to be missed.

"You were looking for me, I suppose," Hilda said.

She thought that Mrs. Frearson's voice ought to be a light, musical treble, immature, like her slender body, and with something of the same awkward, girlish attraction. On the other hand, for all that Hilda knew, Mrs. Frearson might be dumb. To discover that would hardly have been surprising.

What did surprise her was the deep, rough voice, extraordinarily like Miss Perriman's, that came from the small pink mouth in the wax-white face.

"I'm looking for my sister," Mrs. Frearson said.

"Looking for your sister—here?"

Hilda glanced about her, half-expecting Miss Perriman to appear through the gaping hole that led to what had once been Stephen's study, or at the head of what was left of the staircase, or to emerge from the drawing-room, which, as far as Hilda could tell from where she stood, had not been damaged.

"Did she come to see me?" she asked. "We stayed the night at the Lucketts' and only came back to look round a few minutes ago."

"She said she was coming here," Mrs. Frearson answered. "I tried to prevent it, but she insisted on coming, in case she could help."

"That was very kind of her."

"She *is* very kind," Mrs. Frearson said flatly, as if there had been argument on the point, which it was important to silence. "Didn't you see her?"

"I told you," Hilda said, "we've only just arrived."

"I meant last night."

"You mean she came here last night?"

"Of course, of course!" The harsh voice rose shrilly. "She saw the fire, and she insisted on coming, in case she could help. I warned her not to. I said it was dangerous. But you can't stop her helping, when she's made up her mind to it."

"And you mean she never came back?"

"No!" The word rang out accusingly.

As if she felt some menace behind it, Katherine moved closer to Hilda with a protective and rather belligerent look on her face. Just then someone thrust at the door that Hilda had closed behind her. Moving aside, she expected to see Crankshaw come in, but instead it was Nelson.

"Excuse me," he said to Mrs. Frearson. "I overheard what you were saying." He looked very tired, and this gave an appearance of even greater austerity than usual to his long, thin face. "You *are* Mrs. Cater, are you not?" But giving her no time to reply, he turned and said to Hilda, "This is fortunate. I hoped I'd find you, and I was going to propose to you that we should go together and talk to Mrs. Cater and her sister. Now we can talk here. I think you'll find we can sit in the drawing-room in moderate comfort, though it may be rather cold. Naturally there's no electricity."

There was a chill precision in his manner which made it unfamiliar to Hilda. She thought that it must be his professional personality, slipped into automatically when he heard the accusing note in the voice of their uninvited guest.

As she led the way into the drawing-room, Hilda told him, " We came here to see if we could move back to-day. I thought we'd be able to, but I'm afraid I was over-optimistic."

Katherine looked round dispiritedly at the room, which was the one that had suffered the least damage in the house, yet in which grey ash had drifted over everything and the air felt as cold and dank as in a leaky cellar.

" Yes, you were," she said. " But we won't go back to the Lucketts'."

" We'll talk about that later," Nelson said. With his handkerchief, he dusted a couple of chairs. " I'm so glad we've this opportunity to talk to Mrs. Cater before the police take any action, as no doubt they soon will." He thrust a chair towards her, inviting her, as he might have in his own office, to be seated. " You *are* Mrs. Cater? "

She gave a fierce shake of her head.

" Oh, come," he said quietly.

" No, I——"

She stopped. With a small shrug of resignation, she took the chair that he had offered her.

" Yes, I am," she said. " But I'm not a murderess. I didn't murder my husband. I didn't murder that woman in the car. And I didn't murder your brother, Miss Gazeley." The rough voice sounded calm, and the gaze of her wide, china-like eyes, fastened on Hilda, seemed merely a little vacant. But her thin body gave a convulsive shiver. " But who's going to believe me. And what's going to happen to me now? "

If she had burst into tears, Hilda would have felt less moved. The empty look seemed to express a terrible familiarity with those two desperate questions.

" Would you tell us about it? " Hilda suggested. She sat down on another of the dusted chairs, and as much because of the chill of the fear that reached her from the other woman, as because of the chill of the room, drew her coat closely about her. " We know that you couldn't have been here at the time when my brother was killed."

" Do you? And do you actually believe it? " Lucy Cater said bitterly. " Are you so inhuman that you actually believe evidence? That would be something new in my experience."

" Didn't the jury that acquitted you of the murder of your husband believe the evidence? " Nelson asked.

" I don't suppose they did," she answered. " Giving a verdict in accordance with the evidence and believing it in your heart aren't quite the same thing. I long ago gave up the hope that anyone would ever believe any good of me."

" Mr. Wingard told me he thought you'd been rightly acquitted," Hilda said.

" But how did he explain my being alive, except by assuming I'd committed another murder? That woman in the car, that woman who's got a grave-stone over her with my name on it, how did she get where she is unless I put her there? "

Impassively, Nelson answered. " I don't know. How did she? "

" By accident," Mrs. Cater answered defiantly. " My husband died in an accident with a gun. That woman, whoever she was, died in an accident with the car. Accident, accident! Two too many accidents isn't it? Why don't you say so? "

" *Whoever* she——? You mean you don't even know who she was? " Hilda exclaimed.

" I haven't the slightest idea."

" But how could that happen? "

" She stole my car," Mrs. Cater said. " I was on my way to see my sister. I hadn't seen much of her for a long time. We'd never got on very well, even as children, and it was worse when we grew up. You know what she's like. She envied me and disapproved of me. She didn't like my husband. And I thought her domineering and puritanical. But she stood by me when I was arrested, and though she was one of the people who never believed I hadn't killed Clive deliberately, she told me I could always count on her if I needed help. And after the acquittal I needed it badly. I'd no money and nowhere to go and I was ill, and people wouldn't leave me alone. That's to say, some of them wouldn't, the ones who wanted a sensational story out of me, while all the others turned their backs on me. I couldn't get a job. I couldn't get lodgings. So I made up my mind at last that I'd have to go to my sister, at least until I was well enough to face these things again. And I started off for Yorkshire, where she was living then, in my car."

She paused to draw a rasping breath. She was in a state of terror. Hilda realised that all these months while they had had their amusement at her mysteriousness, the woman had been living with terror.

"It's odd how things work out," Mrs. Cater went on. "I nearly sold my car and went by train, but then I thought that a car was really the one way I could get away from everybody. You know what I mean. You get in a car, you slam the door and drive off, and there isn't a soul whose look you've got to meet, or who can say a word to you. So I kept the car. But at a café somewhere beyond Welwyn, where I stopped for a cup of tea—and I was inside for only ten minutes or so—someone stole it. Someone, that woman, stole the car, drove off in it much too fast and wrecked it and was killed. As I told you, an accident!"

"You never notified the police that your car had been stolen, did you?" Nelson said.

"No," she answered.

"Why didn't you?"

"I'd had more than enough of the police."

Katherine, who had not sat down, but had been standing by the empty fireplace, broke in, " I can understand that. I shouldn't have either."

Mrs. Cater gave no response to this expression of sympathy. It might have been as unwelcome to her as a doubt of her story.

" I don't think it even crossed my mind that I ought to tell the police that my car had been stolen," she said. " I remember I stood there in the small car-park, looking at where I knew I'd left the car, and telling myself that it was gone and that the only thing that mattered now was to find out some other way of getting to my sister. And then a bus came by and I got on to it. And presently I changed buses, and at last I got to my sister's house. It was late at night, hours later than she'd been expecting me. She saw me standing in the garden, in the dark, and she gave a sort of scream." Mrs. Cater gave a high laugh. " Yes, she screamed. She'd heard about my death on the radio, and she thought I was a ghost. It's the only time in my life I've seen my sister frightened."

At the best of times, Hilda thought, it would have been easy enough to mistake Mrs. Cater for a ghost, and when the news of her death had just come to one in the official tones of a radio announcer, it would have been an unnerving experience to see her looking in, white-faced, out of the darkness.

" Did you tell her what had happened? " Nelson asked.

" Yes, I did," Mrs. Cater said.

" And didn't she tell you that you must tell the police? "

" She? " Her laugh this time was louder. " You don't seem to understand my sister. All her life she's been utterly bored and utterly reckless. When she was young she used to go rock-climbing, she used to explore caves, she used to go sailing in rough seas—anything for some excitement and danger. But then she had a bad fall and had to give up all those things, so my situation that night was a heaven-sent opportunity to her. It was she who pointed out that I could stay dead if I wanted to."

Springing up, she began to walk about the room with quick, nervous strides. As she went on there was still the same harsh antagonism in her voice, yet she held her hands pressed together before her, in what looked like a gesture of supplication. She might unconsciously have been imploring them to try to understand her.

" Well, at first I didn't know if I wanted to," she said. " More than anything, I'd have liked it if I could really have died. But what happened was that I simply became ill. I was feverish. I had delusions. I couldn't eat. Then at last, when I got better, I found that the whole thing had been decided for me. I *was* still dead. My sister had been to my funeral and ordered a tombstone for me. She'd even paid for the tombstone. It says on it, ' *Requiescat in pace.*' "

She stood still suddenly, looking intently at Nelson.

" Think of it—rest in peace! The peace of a prison, with her as my warder. The life-sentence I thought I'd missed. Of course we had to move away from Yorkshire, and we had to change our names. We moved twice before we came here, each time because she thought someone had recognised me. Yet I hardly ever went out, I saw no visitors, I accepted no invitations. I used just to go for a walk at dusk, as I've done since we came here."

Nelson gave a troubled sigh. " It seems I'm to blame for a good deal, Mrs. Cater. If I hadn't thought I recognised you, and if I hadn't come in and joked about it . . ." He smoothed back some imaginary hair from his bald forehead. " You see, it was I who put it into Stephen Gazeley's head that you were someone in whom it might be worth his while to take an interest, and we don't know just what that may have led to. Now about your sister——"

Mrs. Cater interrupted him swiftly. " I know, you're going to tell me it's ugly to speak of her as I have. You're going to say she's been very kind to me, that if she hadn't taken care of me I'd probably be in a lunatic asylum by now. That's true, that's terribly true. She's been generous and devoted, and perhaps she never thought of it as—as revenge. Her kind don't, you know. They don't question the reasons for their own actions. They're always right, they're always righteous, and if anything goes wrong, someone else is to blame. Well, just for once I'm not accepting the blame." Her grey-blue eyes blazed. For that moment she lost all likeness to a wax image. " I have *not* done wrong! I only did what she told me."

Nelson went on stroking his forehead, looking embarrassed.

" What I was really going to ask you," he said, " was if I heard you correctly, as I arrived here, saying that Miss Perriman hadn't been home all night."

" No, she hasn't," she said.

" And that she came over here yesterday evening to see if she could help at the fire? "

" Yes."

" Though you'd told her it was dangerous."

" Yes."

" Why should you have thought it might be dangerous? " he asked.

" Because——" She faltered for an instant. " Because fires are always dangerous, of course. But she loves danger. It draws her like a magnet. I don't think she'd have been capable of staying away."

" You must have been very worried then, when she didn't come home."

" I didn't know it till this morning. I took my sleeping-pills as usual and went to bed. And you'll say, I suppose, that in the circumstances I can't be certain she didn't come home. That's true, perhaps. Only her bed hadn't been slept in, she hadn't made herself any tea, as she probably would have if she'd come in late, and she certainly hadn't had any breakfast this morning. So I think it's certain that she never came home, and I came here to find out if anyone had seen her, because I'm worried now. I'm very worried."

"Yes," Nelson said thoughtfully. "I think you are."

"Didn't any of you see her?"

He shook his head. So did Hilda.

Katherine, frowning, said, "You said she came over here in the evening. But it was really afternoon still when the fire started. What time did she come?"

"Oh, not when it started," Mrs. Cater said. "She was out then, doing some shopping in Ledslowe. She came back on the bus that gets in at six-forty, and she didn't come over here straight away."

"So it was seven o'clock at least when she got here." Katherine turned to Hilda. "You and I were at the Lucketts' house by then."

"But there were lots of other people here still," Hilda said. "One of them may have seen her. One of the firemen, perhaps."

"I think, Mrs. Cater," Nelson said sombrely, "you'll have to tell this to the police, even if you don't want to."

It was as if he had told her that she ought to plunge her hand into flames. Blind panic stared at them out of her face, and in a couple of swift strides she was at the door.

"You didn't see her, that's all I want to know," she said. "That's all I came here to find out."

"But, Mrs. Cater—Mrs. Frearson——"

"No!"

With a swirl of her long dark coat, she turned and fled.

Katherine, who was still frowning, turning something over in her mind, looked at Nelson and said, " One might almost think you did that on purpose. Of course she'll never go to the police. But I will."

" Oh, God! " Nelson said. " Yes, that was stupid of me."

" *Did* you do it on purpose? " Hilda asked.

" If you would perhaps suggest what purpose it could possibly have served . . . ? "

Hilda sighed. " I'm sorry, Nelson. Yes, Katherine, do go." And as Katherine went out, she added, " Everything I try to think about seems out of focus. Do you think her story of that accident was true? "

" It might have been," he said.

" But you rather doubt it."

He flung himself down in an easy chair, heedless of the little cloud of ash that rose up around him from the cushions.

" I'll tell you something, Hilda," he said. " I've been thinking rather a lot about Miss Perriman, and if the story of that accident isn't true—that's to say, if it was actually a murder of some unknown woman, done to help Lucy Cater to disappear—then I think it was Miss Perriman and not her sister who organised the whole thing. I've no evidence whatever to support it. It's just a guess, to which I feel inclined to give a little more thought than I might have since I've heard Mrs. Cater describe her sister's character. Bored, reckless, attracted by danger . . . To me that sounds like an excellent thumb-nail sketch of a murderess. And yesterday morning Miss Perriman lied—lied most deliberately—about her whereabouts at the time of Stephen's murder."

" You said that yesterday," Hilda said, " but you didn't explain it."

" Don't you remember what she told us about seeing the starlings? She said she was in the garden, doing a little weeding, and she saw an enormous flock of starlings fly past."

" Ah yes," Hilda said, " and she said she didn't really like birds much, but that all the same she thought they looked wonderful against the sunset."

" She said they looked wonderful, flying *into* the sunset."

" Well? "

" Well, it's a fact that starlings come down to roost among the ruins from every direction," Nelson said, " but if she'd been in her garden, the ones she'd have seen flying overhead would have been coming *out of* the sunset. If she really saw starlings flying *into* the sunset, then she was on this side of the ruins, not the other." He struck an arm of his chair with the flat of his hand. Again ash rose in a small cloud about him. " And think of this, Hilda. Stephen made a telephone-call to that house over there on Sunday morning. The exchange has a record of the call and can be trusted rather more than Miss Perriman or her sister, who deny having taken it. Well, what was that call about? Stephen had found out in London, earlier in the week, that Mrs. Frearson was Lucy Cater. Don't you think then that he was ringing up Lucy Cater, telling her he wanted to have a private chat with her, and suggesting that she should interrupt her usual evening walk to call on him, when you would be away at church? And don't you think that she immediately told her sister all about the call, and her sister told her that for once she'd got to drop that evening walk altogether and go into Ledslowe and get herself a good alibi—which she did by picking up an unsavoury character called Stan Brown. That has to be the reason why Mrs. Cater did that—and what she meant just now when she said that she'd only done what her sister told her to. Otherwise her choosing just that evening to break loose is too big a coincidence. And while she was safely out of the way with Brown, Miss

Perriman came over here in her place, and ..." A small gesture of his dusty hand finished the sentence.

"And yet somehow you didn't see her, Nelson," Hilda said.

CHAPTER XIV

It seemed a long time before he answered. At last he said, "No, I didn't. You'll just have to believe me about that, Hilda."

Hilda found it almost impossible to believe it. To cover this fact, she said: "Yes, I suppose I shall. And it was Miss Perriman, I suppose, who tried to search Stephen's room, and knocked me on the head when I interrupted her."

"Well, wasn't it?" Nelson said.

"And came here yesterday afternoon, when she was supposed to be shopping in Ledslowe and set fire to the house, in the hope of destroying whatever it was she hadn't been able to find the night before?"

"It all adds up, you know."

"Except for what she thought she'd find, after the police had been through the place."

"I know—that's the stumbling block." Nelson stood up. He looked down at his clothes and began listlessly patting them to remove some of the dust that they had picked up from the easy chair. "She made quite a good job of the fire, anyway. What are you going to do now, Hilda? You can't stay here."

"No, I think we'll join you in your hotel to-night."

"I don't mean just to-night." He walked to the door and stood looking along the passage towards the devastation at the end of it. "You can re-build this place in time, I suppose."

"I suppose so," Hilda said.

" Do you think you will? "

She was aware of a great reluctance to answer. She had not yet come to terms with her growing sense of relief because her life here was finally ended, and she could not have admitted to Nelson that she actually felt a furtive gratitude for the fire that had hastened the end.

" The house belongs to Katherine," she said. " It'll be for her to decide what's to be done with it."

" She'll do what you want," he said.

" Will she? That hasn't always characterised her behaviour in the past."

" Oh, come. When it's something that's important to you, she will. She's very fond of you." He turned back to look at her intently. " Don't stay here, Hilda. It isn't the life for you."

" Well, I must have time to think," she answered. " It still depends on Katherine."

" She'll soon be married."

" I wish I were sure of that."

" Of course she will be. She and young Luckett are madly in love," he said.

" If they are, some of their ways of showing it are rather curious. Or aren't they? Perhaps I'm hardly the person to judge."

" To which you might add, neither am I," he said. " Only you might be wrong there."

He walked towards her and stood looking down at her as she sat huddled in her coat in the desolate room.

" Come away from here, Hilda. You've done your job. I know you had to do it, and I—I think all the more of you for the way you did it. But don't cling to your burden, particularly one that isn't really there any more. You're still a young woman. You've a life of your own to live."

The words came to her like an echo out of an immeasurably remote past. Yet it was only six years since she had had a life of her own, a life which in retrospect had sometimes seemed to have a charm so intense that she had often been driven to trying to blot it out of her memory.

The library where she had worked for ten years among agreeable, unremarkable colleagues, her small flat in Battersea, the evenings spent with friends or quite pleasantly alone, the occasional theatres and concerts, the short holiday abroad every year, and of course the salary, which had been small but had been hers to spend unquestioned, these had made up a life which had acquired, once she had left it behind, such glamour that there had seemed to be a sort of guilt in thinking about it.

The odd thing was that in those days she had had the habit of thinking of herself as a lonely woman. She had envied her friend Amabel, who had been married to Stephen. The utter loneliness that such a man as he could generate around him had been beyond her imagination.

And even now, when she had experienced it for six years, she found it difficult to recognise that loneliness was what she had suffered. For Stephen, in his way, had certainly loved her, and how can you be lonely if you are well loved? Only, she thought, if you are at heart a thoroughly selfish person, the sort of person who perversely prefers life in a small flat of her own to keeping house for somebody else. Hilda had often brooded on her own selfishness.

"A young woman?" she said, smiling up wryly at Nelson. "I wonder when one stops saying that sort of thing to oneself."

"I hope not until other people stop saying it—and I'm saying it," he said. "I'm saying it in spite of the fact that for the last few years you've been doing your best to turn yourself into someone too old to take any interest in anything but this blasted house—which I'm glad to see in ashes!"

"In ashes is a slight exaggeration," she said.

"Well, I wish it weren't. I wish it were flat on the

ground. I wish——" He stopped, giving a short laugh. "No, what I wish can wait. It's waited long enough already. But I'm going to see you get away from here, Hilda. If you haven't the initiative left to start a quite different sort of life, I'm going to supply it."

He laid a hand on her arm. Yet immediately, as if contact with her had scorched him, he snatched the hand away.

"We seem to be forgetting the rather important question of what's happened to Miss Perriman," he said. "Did she just lose her head and bolt? It seems a little out of character."

With a certain amusement, Hilda recognised the Nelson she knew, the man who fled headlong from his own feelings as soon as he became aware of them.

Unthinkingly she laid her own hand on her sleeve, gently stroking the soft fur where Nelson's hand had lain. She was glad that she had saved the coat from the fire. It was precious, tangible evidence that Stephen had been capable sometimes of tenderness and generosity. The thought would comfort her whenever she felt worst shamed by her own past blindness concerning him.

"I think I should be quite glad to forget Miss Perriman," she said, "and her sister, and a lot of other people too. Particularly, I'd like to be able to forget Inspector Crankshaw. Whenever I think of him, I get a horrible feeling that I've lied to him, and that by now he knows it. The mere thought of him gives me a conscience." She got up and went to the door. "I wonder if Katherine found him."

Behind her, Nelson began, "Hilda, when all this is over . . ."

But his voice hesitated there, and Hilda did not wait to learn how he might make up his mind to finish the sentence.

As she went out into the garden, intending to find Katherine, she thought of suggesting to her that they should go to Ledslowe together, take rooms in the hotel, then go on a shopping expedition, to buy a few clothes. For not only were the clothes indispensable, but it seemed to Hilda that to go shopping would be very good for them both. Choosing stockings and shoes, they might keep their minds off murder for a few minutes. Underwear might exorcise Miss Perriman and her sister. A new hat might blot out the slightly squinting, sharp little eyes of Inspector Crankshaw.

True, Hilda was not certain how she stood for money, but she had an account at one or two shops in Ledslowe, and beyond that, she thought, she could probably borrow from Nelson. And in Ledslowe, away from this house and from all the people who might interfere, Hilda would talk to Katherine about Colin.

Not knowing in which direction Katherine had gone, she stood still outside the front door, and called her.

There was no answer, but in the moment that followed, as she stood there listening and preparing to call again, she heard the unmistakable sound of a spade being driven into the earth, the thump of the clod falling as the spade turned it, and again the spade being driven into the earth. Astonished, she went a few steps farther out into the garden and saw Jim Kent, at work among the vegetables.

He straightened up as she came towards him.

" Good morning, Miss Gazeley," he said. " I hope you're better. I mean after that night. I told Maureen. She said I oughtn't to have left you. She said I ought to've gone for the doctor straight away. She said I ought to've gone for the police. ' You oughtn't to have left her there like that,' Maureen said, ' without even rousing anyone else in the house.' "

" Jim! " Hilda interrupted. It seemed to her that this uncharacteristic flow of words was merely to stop her asking the question she was about to ask, " What are you doing here, Jim? "

"Why, I'm getting the ground ready for the onions, Miss Gazeley," he said. "I'm behind with it. I said to Maureen, 'I don't know whether they'll be staying on after the fire,' I said, 'but it's a pity to let the garden get out of hand. Even if they're going to move away and want to sell the place,' I said, 'they don't want to let the garden get out of hand.'"

"No, Jim—thank you," Hilda said. "But now tell me what you're really doing here. You don't like me. You didn't like my brother. For the last year or so you've looked at us as if we were your bitterest enemies. So what are you doing here to-day?"

He drew the spade out of the ground, suddenly drove it in again sharply and let go of it.

"Well, I came to have a talk with you," he said. "It's been hard, not having anyone I could talk things over with, not even Maureen. Because I couldn't bear to see her worried. The kids mean everything in the world to her. She's been a different woman since we had them. And she's done wonders for them too. They was like scared little rabbits when they come, and look at them now. And they're good kids, they really are, Miss Gazeley, and they're healthy and they think the world of her. It couldn't do them no good if they was to have to go, now could it?"

She heard the increasing tension in his voice, as if the effort of nerving himself to speak were almost too much for him.

"But why should they ever have to go?" she asked. "I can't imagine anyone who'd be better with them than Maureen."

"That's it," he said eagerly. "That's what I think. It's for them as well as for her—though I think she'd go out of her mind if they was taken away. And that's why I never could tell her about the trouble I was having with Mr. Gazeley. Sooner than that, I was ready to do anything, just to keep him quiet, specially as maybe it was my fault in the first place, talking back to him. You don't want to talk back to men like Mr. Gazeley. They don't understand it. But I never could think straight about it, because there was no one I could go to to tell me what I ought to do. And then yesterday Crankshaw had it all out of me and told me I been a fool. I didn't mean to tell him, but he had it all out of me before I knew what I was saying hardly, and he said I been a fool taking any notice of Mr. Gazeley, thinking he could do us any harm, and thinking you ever knew anything about it. So I come to say I was sorry if I seemed unfriendly, and——" He had gone scarlet in the face while he was talking. Grabbing the spade again, he jerked it out of the ground. "And you don't want to let the garden get out of hand," he said and started digging furiously.

"Stop, Jim—please stop," Hilda said. "I've understood hardly a word you've been saying."

With a defiant air, he turned two or three spadefuls, then straightened up once more and eyed her with a stubborn sort of look which made her afraid that she might not be able to get another word out of him.

"Now let's start at the beginning," she said. "You had a quarrel with my brother?"

He nodded.

"What was it about?" she asked.

"Manure."

"Why ever should you quarrel about manure?"

"He wouldn't have me use it. He said we had enough compost here. Well, all right, I said, I've nothing against compost, it's the best thing you can do if you haven't got farmyard, but farmyard's better, and you can get some from Mr. Luckett, I'll be seeing his man, Bert Bendale, I said, and I'll tell him we want half a load. Well then, Mr. Gazeley blew right up in the air. Some of the things he said to me—I couldn't make sense of half of it, but I know he said it wasn't legal for Mr. Luckett to sell the manure when he needed it for his own land.

Well, I said, you don't have to worry about that, there isn't a farmer living who won't take ready cash when he can get it, you give him ready cash, I said, so he doesn't have to fill up a form about it, and Bert'll bring it round."

Jim Kent gave his head a bewildered shake.

"Well, Miss Gazeley, I know he was a lawyer, and a lawyer's got to have respect for the law, and maybe there is some such regulation, even if I never heard of it, but when it's just a matter of half a load of manure between neighbours—well, I couldn't see any reason for him to say the things he did, and so I gave him a piece of my mind back. I don't recall just what I said, but I know I told him I didn't expect him to teach me my job, and maybe I called him a puffed-up little turkey-cock or some such thing. And that's where I went wrong, because a small man can be sensitive about his size. He said I'd better look out, and he said the thing too that made all the trouble. He said if I wasn't careful he'd go to the people at the church-home, the one that sent us the kids, and tell them Maureen and me wasn't fit to look after them."

Only too easily, Hilda could imagine the scene. Stephen insulted, furious, vengeful, might have said anything, even something as cruel as that. Once, however, she would have been certain that he did not mean it. It might have upset her for days, but in the end she would have managed to forget it. Now that almost pleasant time seemed already very long ago.

"But what harm could it have done you, even supposing he'd done such a thing?" she said. "The children themselves are the best proof you could have that it wasn't true."

"Ah, but you don't know the sort of people who run that kind of home," he said. "And you see, Maureen and me ... Well, I told it all to Crankshaw, and he said I didn't have to worry, he knew some of the governors and I'd no reason to be afraid, so now I've started, I'll tell you the lot. You see, when we first came here to live, Maureen and me had just got married. We told them that at the home, and that was all fair and square, we didn't tell no lies. But what we didn't tell them was we'd been living as man and wife for five years before that. Maureen got married when she was only seventeen, and the man run off and left her a year or two later, and she never knew what become of him. So we couldn't get married when we wanted to, and so in the end we went off together, and Maureen called herself Mrs. Kent, and no one where we was knew any better. And then in the end we got the news that the fellow was dead and we got married, and we aren't ashamed of anything. But if the people at the home found out, I thought, they'd maybe think we wasn't fit to look after the children."

"But wait a moment, Jim," Hilda said. "How did my brother find out all this?"

"Why, I don't know, Miss Gazeley."

"He *did* know it, I suppose?"

"He must've, mustn't he? What else could he have said against us to the people?"

"But did he actually say—did he say in so many words —that this was what he was going to say to them?"

Jim Kent rubbed his forehead with his earthy knuckles.

"Well, I'm not sure. No, I don't think he did. But it must've been what he meant, mustn't it?"

"Unless you thought that only because it's what you had on your own mind. It's as Inspector Crankshaw said to me, we've all got our secrets. But did my brother really know yours, Jim? Did he ever say to you that he knew this about Maureen and you, or that it was what he was going to tell the people at the home about you?"

He thought it over, frowning perplexedly. Then he shook his head.

"I don't recall that he ever did, but then what else——?"

"Nothing else!" she said. "Perhaps he never meant to tell them anything. Perhaps he just lost his temper, and said the worst thing that came into his head, but without really meaning it."

There was sympathy in his eyes as he looked at her, but he shook his head again and firmly disposed of her hope that the whole matter might have been a misunderstanding.

"Like I said," he said, "Crankshaw told me I been a fool to take any notice, and that's what he meant, maybe. Maybe he meant it was just my acting up that gave Mr. Gazeley the notion he'd got a hold on me. But when he asked me if Mr. Gazeley ever brought the business up again, and I said, well, I said, you know what it is with a man like Mr. Gazeley, half the time he's talking you don't know what he means. He says things and they may be jokes or they may not, but every time he spoke to me about the children after that, even when he seemed in a good humour, I thought he was reminding me what he could do, if he'd a mind to do it. So when he suggested I might put in extra time and never said a word about paying me for it, well, I toed the line, I did everything he wanted. I put in the extra time, and pretended I liked it. I couldn't stand the sight of him, but I did my best to talk to him as if all was forgiven and forgotten on my part—hoping it would be on his."

Hilda was feeling sick. It was far worse than she had ever dreamed, even after she had heard the Lucketts' story.

"I think it was really all a great mistake on your part," she said unsteadily. "I think he only lost his temper violently about the manure—you see, he and Mr. Luckett were on very bad terms, that must have been the reason for that—and perhaps he said the horrible thing that he did without ever really meaning it, and without really believing that you'd take it seriously. And afterwards he probably forgot all about it. That's what he was like—I mean, that's what I always thought he was like. . . ." She knew it was untrue and could not go on.

After a moment, in a voice that sounded colder, only through the effort she had to make to control it, she said, " And that evening when you came in and found me unconscious, what were you really doing out so late, Jim? Did you tell Inspector Crankshaw about that? "

" That was what brought him along to see me," he answered. " Hearing from you about how I found you. And I told him—well, I told him all this, because what I was really doing that night was prowling around, wondering if I could get in and see if there was anything in writing about Maureen and me that could make trouble for us. But it was just a thought in my mind like. I couldn't sleep, and I couldn't talk to Maureen, and I thought I'd go out and look around. And then I seen the light on and I wondered about that and I went close to see. . . ."

He stopped, turning his head at the sound of a car stopping in the road.

It was Colin's car. Colin got out of it, slammed the door and came towards Hilda. He said, " I've come for Katherine. Where is she? "

CHAPTER XV

SOMETHING IN Colin's tone made Jim Kent pick up his spade and walk away.

But Colin did not seem to mind who heard him. He did not lower his voice to say, " I've come to my senses, and I've got to find Katherine."

" She went to look for Inspector Crankshaw," Hilda said. " We had a visit from Mrs. Frearson this morning. She said Miss Perriman came here last night, to see if she could help at the fire, and then never went home again. Katherine went to tell the inspector about it."

Colin was not interested in Miss Perriman. The experience of coming to his senses was of more moment to him than anything else could be.

"I've made a lot of trouble through my stupidity," he said, "and I've got to put it right as quickly as I can. My father explained that to me this morning. He's got a lot more sense than I have."

"Well, time's on his side. It makes a difference," Hilda said mildly.

But Colin was not interested in time either. All his thoughts seemed to be concentrated on one point, and anything that Hilda said seemed likely to affect him only as rather meaningless punctuation in what he himself intended to say. He was quite without his usual cool poise. He was tense and flushed, filled with an excitement which he could barely control.

"It's incredible what a fool one can be," he declared.

"Katherine will come back here," Hilda said. "I don't expect she'll be long. Meanwhile, if all this is just about the murder, and not your relations with Katherine, you might explain some of it to me. Shall we go inside?"

Without saying either yes or no to this suggestion, he started to walk towards the house. But then he turned on his heel and walked back again. Hilda kept at his side, and so found herself walking up and down quickly on the lawn between the house and the kitchen garden.

He had started talking rapidly. She doubted if he quite knew to whom it was he was talking. Speech poured out of him as most likely it had when he was alone in his car, on his way here.

"I started it all when I rushed to Katherine with that story that Mr. Gazeley had been blackmailing my mother," he said. "I'd like you to understand how that happened. I mean, why I didn't stop and think. I'm quite accustomed, you see, to subtracting a good deal from what my mother tells me. She exaggerates, she dramatises, she makes everything more than life-size. Yet I always find her incredibly convincing. She used the word blackmail. She used it and I lost my head and thought she meant it. And I went to Katherine and threw the word at her without any explanations. I wasn't really thinking what it would mean to her. I knew she didn't care much for her father, and it never occurred to me that it would hurt her terribly. But of course it did. It's incredible, it's unforgivable that I shouldn't have known it would hurt her. I was only thinking about the shock I'd had myself that morning, and wanting her to hold my hand for me till I'd got over it."

"But this blackmail, Colin," Hilda said. "What did Stephen do to your mother if he didn't blackmail her?"

"Oh, he scared her. He lost his temper with her and threatened her. He said he'd go to my father and tell him the truth about her. But he didn't demand money with menaces—that's what blackmail is, isn't it? And in fact he never did tell my father anything."

"He scared her... He lost his temper... He threatened..." That was a Stephen Hilda knew, a vicious caricature of a child in a tantrum. There was no difficulty in visualising a scene between him and Valerie in which he had done all those things. "Only I'm not sure that blackmail would be any worse than that," she said. "Did your father tell you all this?"

"Yes—it's the first time we've talked much since that morning," Colin said. "I've rather been avoiding him. I didn't mean to exactly, but I couldn't help it. But this morning he insisted on talking about what had been going wrong between Katherine and me. He loves Katherine, you know. And when I told him that she hated me for saying that her father was a blackmailer,

he told me what had really happened. And so you see
 . . ." He flung out a gesticulating hand again.
" I see," Hilda said thoughtfully. She was thinking
that whatever sort of man Colin's true father might have
been, he had been singularly fortunate in the man who
had acted as his substitute.

Then, all at once, a quite different thought occurred
to her.

She found herself imagining the scene between Arthur
and Colin, the scene from which Colin had come hurrying
out to find Katherine. It could have happened just as
Colin had told her. On the other hand, it could be that
by now the Lucketts had recognised that the story of
Stephen's blackmailing could be a boomerang and that
it might really be advisable to change it a little. No
blackmail, no motive for murder. Only it seemed to
Hilda that there was not a great deal of difference between
demanding money with menaces, and merely doing some
menacing. Perhaps merely to threaten exposure was a
little less calculating, and an argument might perhaps be
made that it had not been meant seriously. But still it
seemed as callously destructive of human happiness.
Besides that, at the time of the murder, Colin at least had
entirely believed the story of blackmail.

" Will you tell me something else? " she said. " Why
haven't you admitted that it was you in the car that drove
past here just after your father and I discovered Stephen's
body? "

" But I have," he said. " I told the police this morning.
That's why I didn't see you at breakfast. I'd gone into
Ledslowe. But my not doing it before was all part of
the same stupidity, really, because, after Katherine and
I separated that morning, I got the feeling there wasn't
another human being I could stand seeing, so I drove
off to the downs, and left the car and went walking.
I've always done that when I got myself in a mess. It's
the nearest thing I've ever discovered to being com-

pletely alone. You can see for miles all round you. No one can come up on you suddenly. No one can surprise you. You've time to sort things out without being interrupted half-way through."

Hilda nodded. She was remembering Valerie's description of Colin. She had said that the first thing he thought of when he had had a shock was that he must hide that fact from others. To that extent, then, Valerie understood her son. He had taken his shock that day to the bare slopes of the downs, and hidden it under the open sky.

"Mind you," he went on, "you don't necessarily arrive at anything, but at least you have time to calm down. I did calm down more or less and decided that I'd got to come back and find Katherine and tell her—well, I'm not sure what I intended to tell her. I think I had some idea of suggesting that we should simply clear out together. It seemed the best thing to do. Then we could both of us forget about our families, I thought, and start clean. So I drove back and came here. And then that damned thing happened. I mean, I saw the one person I couldn't face just then—my father. Just as I was driving up to the house, I saw him standing at the window of your brother's room."

"Yes, that was how it happened," Hilda said. "He went straight to the window. I——" She had gone straight to Stephen, knelt beside him, felt for his heart. "I only went out there after I'd seen you drive past."

"Well, Father looked rather strange," Colin said, "and it was strange too seeing him there at all. I thought he and Mr. Gazeley must have been having a row. So I speeded up and drove straight on. In the mirror, just before I got to the corner, I saw you both come out together. If I'd known what had really happened, I'd have stopped—I *think* I'd have stopped—but all I could think of at the time was that there didn't seem to be a hope of seeing Katherine alone just then, and a family row, a row of any sort, seemed to me something there wasn't any reason to endure. Can you understand that?"

That hardly needed a reply. In the future that Hilda was tentatively beginning to plan for herself, the future of a small flat, and an unambitious job, there were to be no rows. Just a squabble or two now and then to keep one human, but a full-scale row, even if it didn't quite lead to murder—never!

"All the same, why didn't you tell anyone all this before this morning?" she asked.

"Oh, I did," Colin answered. "I told my mother. Father telephoned some time that evening with the news of the murder, and it took her about two seconds to make up her mind that I'd done it, because of what she'd told me in the morning. And when I told her about having driven past the house and been seen by you, she nearly had hysterics. But she so completely refused to believe my story of what I'd really been doing there that I got scared, and began to think she was right when she advised me not to admit to anyone that I'd been the driver of the car. She said Father wouldn't give me away, and that you couldn't possibly be certain, at that distance, that you'd seen me. And it wasn't as if I'd seen anything, while I was passing, that could help the police——"

"Colin—wait a moment!" All at once there were half a dozen questions that Hilda wanted to ask him. "You really didn't see anything? You didn't see anyone come out of the house a moment before your father?"

"No."

She stood still. "So it *was* at the back of the house..."

There was not much point in going on. Colin, keeping up his swift walking up and down, had not stood still when she had, and by now was yards ahead of her. Also, at that moment, Katherine and Nelson appeared round the corner of the house.

Colin went straight to Katherine. He grasped her tightly by the arms. He had forgotten Hilda. He did not notice Nelson.

" I came for you—it's got to stop, all the nonsense, it's got to stop—now," Colin said.

" Don't," Katherine said, trying to draw away from him. If he could ignore their audience, she was intensely aware of them. " Something's happened, Colin. Miss Perriman——"

He interrupted, " Listen, you're coming away with me now. We'll drive up to the downs. We'll forget all this for a while. Come along."

" But we can't—not now! "

" Go along, Katherine," Nelson said, and gave her a little push towards Colin. " There's no need for you to stay around here. And I'm going to take Hilda out to lunch in Ledslowe."

" Fine! " Colin said enthusiastically. " Enjoy yourselves! "

With an arm round Katherine, he started to hustle her towards the gate. She looked round at Hilda, seeming near tears, but then suddenly she smiled brilliantly, gave up her resistance and went running with Colin to the car.

Hilda stood looking after them. As they drove off together she was shocked to discover that the thought uppermost in her mind was that it was going to take some getting used to, the business of living alone again. It might be comfortable, it might be peaceful, but it might not be just the easiest thing in the world to become accustomed to not being needed.

She turned to Nelson. " What's the news about Miss Perriman? " she asked.

" Only that there isn't any," he said. " She's vanished."

" Have you been speaking to the inspector about it? "

" Yes, and at the moment there's no confirmation that she ever arrived here yesterday evening, to look on at the fire. But he's had no time yet to investigate. Now let's forget about her and drive into Ledslowe and have the best lunch we can find. And don't say you couldn't touch it, because it'll do you more good than anything else could, particularly if we have a couple of drinks first, and take our time about it."

"Very well," Hilda said, " and afterwards I think I'll do some shopping."

" That sounds an excellent idea."

" Only you may have to lend me some money for it."

" Name your sum."

With his arm through hers, he drew her towards the gate.

Hilda was pleased and grateful. Though it was with deep relief and thankfulness that she carried with her the memory of the look that had been on the faces of Katherine and Colin, as they had driven away together in Colin's small car, she was chilled by sadness which would have made her welcome just then even an explosion of bad temper from Stephen in one of his worst moods.

She and Nelson had lunch at the Dragon, the hotel where Nelson had stayed the night. It was a hot, stodgy, comforting meal of steak-and-kidney pudding and baked apples and custard. Before it they drank sherry in the quiet bar and with the meal had a bottle of Burgundy. Their talk at first, by an effort, was of anything that they could think of other than the murder. Nelson gave it as his opinion that this would do them both good, and whenever the murder threatened to slip into what they were saying, he gave the conversation a determined jolt on to some new track, and Hilda did her best to co-operate. But the result was an unusual constraint, until, with the wine, they began to forget their vigilance, and to talk of what inescapably dominated their minds.

It seemed to come naturally after an unimportant reminiscence of Hilda's about her childhood, for after an hour's careful avoidance of his name, she had at last mentioned Stephen. A short silence followed, but then there seemed to be nothing for her to say but that in her whole lifetime, she had never given Stephen as much thought as she had in the past two days.

"I've thought and thought and tried to understand him," she said. "I've tried to imagine what satisfaction it can have given him to treat some people as he did. But it doesn't make any sense to me. In a way I'd understand better if he'd done it for money. Simple blackmail for profit—after all, that's quite rational. But merely trying to spoil people's lives because, I suppose, they'd offended him somehow, that's beyond me. Particularly as at the same time he could be affectionate and kind."

"That isn't uncommon in the worst criminals," Nelson said. "The only thing is, you can't rely on it. You never can tell when some odd spin of the coin is going to show you the reverse side of it. But how do you know he never did it for money?"

"He didn't with the Lucketts, or with Jim Kent. Do you know about Jim, Nelson?" She told him the story that she had been told that morning. Even in the telling, it made her again feel slightly sick. But a gulp of wine steadied her, releasing an unfamiliar glow of anger. "It was worse, much worse, than what he tried to do to Valerie."

"Only because it succeeded," Nelson said.

"But that's what I mean. It succeeded because Jim's ignorant and vulnerable. He didn't dare to talk it over with anybody. But Valerie was clever enough to go straight to her husband, so Stephen lost his power over her. It was attacking someone as helpless as Jim that was so despicable."

"I don't see any difference in the intent," Nelson said. "Stephen misjudged Valerie's character, but for all you know, it was his intention to bleed her white, and perhaps drive her to suicide. And that's what he probably meant to do to Lucy Cater—what he would have done, if he hadn't run into—well, trouble."

" Trouble from Miss Perriman? " Hilda said.

" Perhaps," he answered.

" You don't feel sure? "

" Why should I? "

" Because of her disappearance."

" Meaning she lost her nerve and bolted, or possibly killed herself, all to save her sister? "

" Why not? " Hilda said. " Isn't it the likeliest explanation? "

He reached for the bottle and tipped some more wine into his glass.

" I don't know, perhaps it is," he said. " Only it won't have saved her sister from anything. Her identity was bound to come out, if a murder inquiry started up in the neighbourhood, and then questions were bound to follow about how that other woman died in the car. But still, I suppose it's possible that Miss Perriman didn't think things out as far as that. She could be the murderess."

" Surely you know whether she is or not, Nelson."

" What do you mean? "

" Didn't you see her—or someone else—come out at the back of the house and throw the hoe in the river? "

" I told you——"

" I know you did." Hilda drank some more wine. " And I don't believe you. Neither does Inspector Crankshaw."

As Nelson pushed his chair back from the table, Hilda thought that he was going to get up and leave her. But even if that had been his first thought, he changed his mind and only twisted his spare body sideways, leaning an elbow on the table.

" Hilda, I think I'm going to tell you a story," he said. " It's a story I hate to tell, but when you know it, you'll understand, I hope, why I didn't see anyone come out at the back of the house. It goes back about four years.

Does that mean anything to you? Do you remember anything that happened about four years ago? "

" I'll remember all sorts of things, if I start trying," she said.

" This was something unusual."

" Well then. . ." But for some reason, the only thing that she could think of at first was that her fur coat, thrown off now, over the back of her chair, was about four years old, and though the gift of the coat from Stephen had been distinctly unusual, she did not think that that could be what Nelson meant. Stephen had made her that present to comfort her at a time when he believed that Nelson had treated her badly, and she did not see how Nelson, even if he had ever connected the two events, could hold that against him.

After thinking of the coat, however, she remembered suddenly that there had been a long time when Nelson's visits had stopped. For more than a year he had not come near them. At the time she had been certain that it had been herself whom he had been avoiding. But suppose that had been a mistake.

" Did you and Stephen have a quarrel? " she asked.

If they had, and if Stephen had blamed himself for Nelson's flight, it explained the gift of the coat.

" Well yes, we had a quarrel," Nelson answered. He was looking at her hard, pulling at his long chin. " Do you know what it was about? "

" You had so many quarrels. I never took much notice of them."

" But what did you think they were about? "

" Oh, I don't know. Chess, I suppose. They always seemed to happen when you were playing chess."

Nelson gave a loud laugh. He brought his fist down on the table so that their glasses rocked.

" They were about you, Hilda. Did you really never know that? "

CHAPTER XVI

HILDA'S EYES widened slightly as she returned his look.

"No," she said sharply, "and I don't believe it."

"You can believe it, it's true. Four years ago Stephen realised that I'd fallen in love with you, and that I was meaning to ask you to marry me. One evening, when we were playing chess, he asked me if that wasn't so. I said it was. I never dreamt my old friend Stephen would have any objection. But he told me then that if I ever thought of trying to take you away from him, he'd go straight to the police with a certain piece of information about me. It was information on how, on a certain occasion, I'd covered up a crime, falsifying some evidence to save a client to whom I'd a peculiar obligation. And the joke of it was that I'd given Stephen that information myself, asking his advice, and that I'd actually acted in the way he suggested. I've often wondered since if he didn't advise me as he did purely to have a hold on me. However, I don't know about that. What I do know is that that evening he threw it up at me and with the most vicious selfishness that I've ever encountered, used it to smash up every hope I'd had of happiness. What, if anything, he smashed for you at the same time, I don't know, but I'd thought, and he certainly must have feared, that you cared for me at least a little."

There was silence when he had ended. Hilda dropped her eyes, looking at the things on the table, a salt-cellar, a small wine-stain on the tablecloth, a piece of bread. She saw them all as from a very long way off.

At last she said, "Why are you telling me this now, Nelson?"

"I told you before I started," he answered. "So that

you should understand why I saw nobody come out of that back door."

" You mean you're again covering up a crime. You're deliberately shielding his murderer, because you're glad he was murdered."

There was another silence.

Hilda raised her eyes again and looked at Nelson. Like the things on the table, his long, sober face with the observant eyes seemed far away. It made her feel dizzy.

" But why did you pretend you'd made it up with him? " she asked. " Why did you start coming here again? "

In a voice that was quiet, but grated with rage, he said, " Because he told me to come, Hilda. It wasn't much fun for him, what he'd done, unless he could see the results occasionally. Apart from that . . . Well, you were here."

" No," she said. " No, that can't be true, that's too much."

" Not too much for Stephen."

" Yes—if he asked you to come here again, I think it was because he thought it was all over and forgotten. He was like that. He never understood the consequences of his actions."

Nelson gave his head a shake. " He understood."

With hasty, fumbling gestures, Hilda began to put on her coat. Her hands were shaking and could not find their way into the sleeves. The waiter came and helped her.

" And Miss Perriman? " she said, as the man went away again. " What about her? "

" I told you," Nelson said, " I didn't see anyone. It was dusk and I was watching you and Luckett. Nothing else can possibly be proved."

" I meant," she said, " suppose Miss Perriman turns up murdered. Suppose she didn't kill Stephen, but only saw who did, and suppose she hasn't bolted or committed suicide, but has been killed herself—what are you going to do then, Nelson?"

"That's something I haven't quite decided."

"I don't understand you," she said. "I still don't really understand why you've told me all this."

"Oh, Hilda——" he began.

She stood up swiftly. "I'm going shopping," she said. "I don't want to go on borrowing Valerie's things, and I've nothing to wear but what I'm standing up in. So I'll go now and see what I can find. I'll see you again some time this evening, I expect."

Before he could speak again, she hurried away. She still felt dizzy, and was afraid of stumbling, but she walked as fast as she was able between the other tables and out into the lobby. As she left the hotel and walked off along the pavement, she remembered that she had intended to borrow money from Nelson for her shopping. That had been an easy thing to suggest an hour before, but no longer felt even possible.

But all that that meant was that she must do her shopping at the one big store in Ledslowe, where she had an account. She shopped hurriedly and carelessly, buying stockings and underwear, a toothbrush and cosmetics, then, realising that this had taken her hardly any time, she went wandering through the other departments, including the furniture and kitchenware, trying to look as if she were thinking of buying a sideboard or a sink-unit. Then, when her feet were too tired for any more of this, she went up to the café on the top floor and ordered a pot of tea.

It was from her window table that she saw the newsboys come out with the evening papers. One took up his stand on the opposite side of the street and started to shout at the uninterested passers-by. Mingled with the noise of the traffic, what he was shouting was unintelligible, and Hilda was paying no more attention to him than to buses and bicycles in the street, till in a lull in the traffic, his words reached her with sudden, complete clarity. Indeed, they were so clear that she thought that it must have been out of her own brain that they had come, and not out of that straining throat.

"Woman's body found in river! Woman's body found in river!"

Hilda picked up the teapot on the table before her and poured herself another cup of tea. With surprise she noticed that her hand was quite steady, which it had not been a few minutes earlier. At the same time, she suddenly became extraordinarily aware of her surroundings, of the big room filled with small tables, the other women drinking tea, the gossiping waitresses, the hum of voices and the clatter of crockery. It was a little like the feeling of coming out from under an electric hair-dryer and it made her realise that for the last hour or two she had been existing in a strange, roaring emptiness, created around her by her own whirling thoughts.

In that moment of steadiness, she asked herself the question that had troubled her most during her talk with Nelson. What had been his real reason for telling her what he had? Why had he deliberately informed her that he had had one of the best of all motives for the murder of Stephen?

That Nelson, of all people, might have been one of Stephen's victims was something that had never once occurred to her, and so far as she could see, there had not been the slightest need for him to enlighten her. So why had he done it?

There was another question too, to which he had given her an answer that had both terribly distressed and failed to convince her. That was the question of why he had resumed his visits to Stephen. Nelson had told her that Stephen had used his hold over him to force him to come for all those week-ends, for the long talks that had usually seemed friendly, for the games of chess. Nelson had also said that Hilda herself had been an inducement.

Picking up her teaspoon, Hilda gave her tea a sudden and vigorous stir, though she never took sugar.

Nelson in love with her all these years, enduring bitter humiliation just to be near her, and then in fact spending all his time painting birds on the other side of the river.

She put the teaspoon down again with a clatter.

Yet then what else had brought him? And why had he told her that he had been blackmailed by Stephen?

Could it be that he had merely wanted her to know the truth about him, feeling that she must know it if the relationship between them was to grow into something rather more important than it had been before? But if so, she had made as many mistakes in her reading of his character as she had in Stephen's. And no doubt she had, so that was no argument against that particular answer to the question. But were there no other answers that would do as well, and perhaps put less of a strain on her credulity?

Nelson had still denied that he had seen the murderer come out at the back of the house, but he had hardly troubled to make his denial convincing. He had seemed to accept the fact that on that point Hilda had made up her mind. Sticking to his earlier story had probably been mainly a precaution against being quoted as having made any definite admission. But it had also been a way of making it clear to Hilda that he did not intend to tell anyone whom he had seen. Realising that, she wondered if she had arrived at the explanation of why he had told her of his own experiences at Stephen's hand. Had it been a way of pleading with her for some sympathy with the murderer?

Until her talk with Nelson over lunch, Hilda had dismissed the possibility that he had been deliberately protecting anyone, because she had thought that the only people in the neighbourhood whom he knew well enough even to think of protecting were herself and Katherine. But then he had let her know that whoever had killed

Stephen had only done something that he might have done himself if he had dared, had done something that had lifted a black cloud of dread from his life and set him free. That person might be someone whom he knew as little as he had known Miss Perriman, or someone whom he had never seen in his life before, but in any case was his friend, with a natural right to his protection.

However, the murderer was not Miss Perriman. She had been found dead in the river. She was a second victim. And what would that mean to Nelson? What would he do now? Would he still sympathise with the man or woman who had taken her frustrated, unrewarded, but devoted life?

But as she thought of that, Hilda wondered why on earth she should be assuming that Miss Perriman had been murdered? Wasn't it still the most likely thing that it was she who had murdered Stephen, and that she had then killed herself? Killed herself perhaps after a talk with Nelson, after the fire, and being told by him that she had given herself away by her blunder about the flight of the starlings into the sunset?

Yet how could Miss Perriman have been the person whom Nelson had seen come out at the back of the house and throw the hoe in the river? Until she had made her mistake about the birds, he had not seemed to know that she had been near the house. So perhaps, after all, she was victim, not murderess, killed because, like Nelson, she had been a witness of the murder, or at least of the murderer's escape, and it was someone else whom Nelson had seen.

Unless he had not seen anybody.

Could that possibly be the truth?

Collecting her parcels, Hilda turned, caught the eye of her waitress, paid her bill, stood up and started to the door.

Could it be the truth that Nelson had seen no one because there had been no one to see? In that case, it was Colin who was lying. For if both of them were telling the truth, then it could only mean that the murder had not happened at the time when she knew that it had happened, that the scream that she and Arthur had heard had not come from Stephen, or even from the study at all, that the french window had not been flung open by the murderer, and that none of the things on which her whole picture of the crime had been built was true.

Perhaps really it had happened earlier, and the scream and the crash been manufactured by some mysterious apparatus. In that case Lucy Cater, with her alibi fixed up for later in the evening, might be the guilty one. Or it might be Arthur Luckett, waylaying Hilda on her way to church, and taking her back to sit where she could conveniently listen to the apparatus do its work, then rushing into the room ahead of her, snatching it and tossing it out to his son, who, by arrangement, was passing at that moment in his car. And the fire, in that case, would of course have been set in order to destroy some little clue to the nature of this noise-making apparatus which it had been impossible to remove. . . .

Hilda had reached the lift. As the metal gate opened before her, she went in like a sleep-walker. The dizziness and the sense of being all alone with the roaring sound made by the whirling of her own poor brain had returned.

She told herself to stop it. She told herself that if she had never been particularly brilliant, she had always had enough common sense not to make too much of a fool of herself, and that instead of spinning fantasies about a noise-making apparatus and trying to incriminate kind, innocent Arthur, or unfortunate Lucy Cater, it would be far better to leave all such things to the intimidating competence of Inspector Crankshaw, and to start worrying a little about what was happening now to Mrs. Cater, that forlorn soul, whose sister had been found dead in the river.

Hilda looked at her watch. If she hurried, she could

catch a bus that would drop her near to Mrs. Cater's house. Emerging into the street, she turned to the left, walking fast towards the bus station. On the way she bought a paper. But she did not try to open it until she was in the bus, and there, sharing a seat with a very stout woman, and trying to hold all her parcels safely on her lap, to find her reading-glasses in her handbag and to put them on, and to open the paper without hitting her neighbour in the face, it was some minutes before she was able to read the news item in the stop-press, which had been shouted up to her by the strident voice of the newsboy.

When she did so, it was only the first few words that she read, then the red type swam before her.

"Found dead in river, woman identified as Mrs. Valerie Luckett. . . ."

CHAPTER XVII

THE BUS STOPPED near Mrs. Cater's house, but Hilda did not move. She did not move until it reached the cross-roads near her home, then she got up, moving stiffly, as if she were in pain, and started slowly up the road.

The sun was low in the sky by the time that she reached the house. It showed round and red between heavy bars of blue-black cloud, and drew her round the ruined end of the house, to sit on the bench there, and, as she so often had before when she needed peace, watch the great flocks of starlings come home to roost in the elms that stood among the jagged walls of the older ruin.

But of course there was nothing left of the bench now but some charred and splintered wood, flattened to the ground under a heap of bricks that had once been a chimney.

However, it was not impossible to sit down on the

bricks, and if she did that for a little while, Hilda thought, she would then be quite ready to go away and never come back again. Indeed, she would far sooner do that than ever return here, and the fact that she would certainly have to come back more than once, to sort out what could be saved of her possessions, was something very much to be regretted. It would be pleasantest simply to sit and watch the starlings wheel home across the burning sky, then go away, taking with her a peaceful memory of a skyful of birds and a quiet river.

She tried not to think about Valerie Luckett, and what had happened to her and why. Presently she would have to go on to the Lucketts' house. There might be something that she could do for Arthur, who had tried to do what he could for her, and she must see Katherine as soon as possible. Then the police would probably have some questions to ask her, though heaven knew what she could tell them.

Valerie had feared that her son would be suspected of Stephen's murder, Valerie had feared that her son had done the murder.... How could one say such things?

But sitting here quietly, one could watch the widening band of light in the west, while overhead a greenish tinge came into the sky, melting into a pale copper radiance above the glow of the sunset.

" Good evening, Miss Gazeley."

Hilda's body jerked. She had heard no one come. Yet there, standing beside her now, dark and massive against the brilliance of the sky with his shadow lying long across the grass, was Inspector Crankshaw.

Hilda managed to reply, " Good evening, Inspector."

He squatted down beside her on a heap of bricks. As he did so, his shadow shrank towards him, lying squat and dark at his feet.

" I'd been hoping I'd find you," he said. " May I ask where you vanished to? "

His voice was friendly and the question not a demand.

"I went out to lunch in Ledslowe with Mr. Wingard," Hilda answered, "then I went shopping." She held out the evening paper to him. "I've only just seen—this."

"Ah, I see," he said.

"Why did you want to see me?"

"Oh, for the usual reason—to ask questions." He turned his head to look at the sunset. "It's very nice here. A lovely view. But aren't you cold, sitting here? The evenings are getting pretty chilly."

"No, I've got my coat, I'm not cold," she said. "And I like it here. I've always liked sitting here. Somehow, it's the one part of the whole house and garden that always seemed to belong to me ... Inspector?"

"Yes, Miss Gazeley."

"What happened to Mrs. Luckett? Did she throw herself in the river?"

"You're thinking that perhaps she'd killed your brother, then committed suicide when she realised her son was going to be suspected?"

Hilda felt a chill down her spine. "Well, I wondered."

He shook his head. "She didn't commit suicide. She was murdered, like your brother. She went out early this morning to meet the murderer, and tell him, I believe, that if her son was suspected, she would tell us what she knew. And so he beat her skull in with a large stone and pushed her body in among some rushes down below the bridge there, where we mightn't have found it as soon as we did if we hadn't been looking for Miss Perriman."

Hilda did not answer for a moment, then she exclaimed, "Oh, look!"

For the starlings had come and the sky was full of a flickering of black wings. They streamed across it towards the round golden ball of the sun, then wheeled down on to the trees, motionless in the still air of the evening.

"That's what I come for," she said. "It's so strange, isn't it? They come from every direction every evening and settle on just that group of trees."

"Like they do at the Marble Arch," Crankshaw said. "I know—I've noticed it."

"And until the last few nights, Mrs. Cater always came by about now. Katherine and I used to say you could set your watch by her."

"That poor woman." He gave a sigh. "I usually say people make their own ill luck, but sometimes one's got to wonder.... If her car hadn't been stolen that day——"

"So her car *was* stolen?" Hilda said.

"Oh yes. We've made inquiries. There was a queer incident the manageress of the café where it happened remembered. A young woman came in for tea, then went out and got hysterical because her car had been stolen. But as soon as the manageress suggested calling the police, the young woman ran out and jumped on to a bus that happened to stop there. No, Lucy Cater isn't a murderess. And as I was going to say, if her car hadn't been stolen that day, when she was on her way to see her sister, she might never have thought of trying to disappear. And if she hadn't thought of that, and if she and her sister hadn't changed their names and started going from place to place till they ended up here, your brother might never have been murdered."

"Then it *was* Miss Perriman who did the murders," Hilda said.

Crankshaw shifted his weight on the bricks, grimacing as the corner of one stuck into him.

"Why no," he said. "Whatever made you think that? They've just vanished again, that's all. Didn't you know that? I think Miss Perriman realised she knew rather too much for her own safety, but didn't want to co-operate with us. And if you ask me why, I think the answer is that if she'd done so, she'd have lost all her power over her sister. So she sent her sister over here this morning to tell her story, so that we'd stop bothering about her, and to start us hunting for Miss Perriman's murdered body, and while we were busy at it, the two of them slipped quietly away. We'll find them, I suppose, if we try hard enough." He looked towards the empty house, where no light shone this evening. "That won't be my job, though, I'm rather glad to say."

Hilda leant towards him tensely. "But you know who did the murders, don't you?"

"Well, it's all quite plain really," he said, "though I don't say it wouldn't have been easier if you hadn't misled me from the start. It was just a little thing you said, and I don't suppose you thought about it one way or the other, but still it would have been easier if you'd told me the same story two days ago as you did this morning.... Are you sure you aren't cold, Miss Gazeley? You look cold."

She gave her head a shake, though her hands, pressed together, were icy. She remembered the feeling that had recurred again and again ever since her first meeting with Crankshaw, the feeling that she had somehow vitally misled him. But she had never intended to do so, and had no memory of what she might have said that could have had that result.

She started to ask what her false statement had been, but Crankshaw cut across her question with one of his own, sharp and unexpected.

"Miss Gazeley, to your knowledge, did Mr. Wingard ever lend your brother money?"

She looked at him blankly, her mind moving at its slowest.

He went on, "I'll tell you why I'm asking. Among the papers we removed from your brother's room on

Sunday night were the statements he had had from his bank, covering the last few years. Also there were diaries, the kind in which he jotted down appointments. And we found that about four years ago Mr. Wingard paid your brother the sum of three hundred pounds. I've asked Mr. Wingard about it, and he says it was a personal loan."

" Then perhaps it was," Hilda said.

" But you don't know anything about it? "

" No."

" And the day after he received this sum," Crankshaw said, " your brother paid out almost the same amount to a furrier in Ledslowe, I think for that very nice coat you're wearing now. And after that it was quite a long time before Mr. Wingard came again on another visit— more than a year. We found that from the diary. So you might almost say it looks as if they'd quarrelled. And knowing that your brother was rather inclined to exert, well, pressure on people—Jim Kent for instance —you might say there was a faint smell of blackmail about. Do you know anything about that, Miss Gazeley? "

In the distance specks stirring in the sky were starlings, visiting from tree to tree before they finally settled down for the night.

Hilda's hand slid over the fur that was wrapped over her knees. She knew now why Nelson had told her what he had that morning. It was because Crankshaw had been to him already, and would, Nelson knew, be coming to her soon with these very questions that he was asking. Nelson had wanted to win her sympathy before Crankshaw could stir up a different sort of feeling. But he had not told her that Stephen had extorted money from him, money with which Stephen had bought her coat, her precious coat.

She shivered inside it. What had made Stephen do that? He had not needed the money. If he had wanted to give her a present, he could easily have afforded to do so. But the coat, worn by her, would always have been a reminder to Nelson that she was not for him. Had that been Stephen's reason?

"They often quarrelled," she said. "I—I don't know why. They seemed to make friends again."

"Are you sure they really did?"

"Well, I'm fairly sure of my brother," she said. "He was like that. He never seemed to realise that people would remember the injuries he'd done them. He did them in rage, then he'd forget them, or so I always thought. I—I'm not sure about Mr. Wingard. I'm not sure why he started his visits again."

"He had two reasons," Crankshaw said. "One was that he'd met and started a love-affair with Valerie Luckett, and when he was supposed to be out alone painting birds, it was easy for them to meet. There were plenty of local people who knew about that, though not, I think, her husband or son. The other, and I think the more important reason was that he'd made up his mind to murder your brother, and he was ready to wait patiently for a time when he thought he could do so safely. It was when he saw Lucy Cater that he decided the time had come."

Violently Hilda exclaimed, "But that's impossible!"

Her mind had skipped what he had said about Valerie and Nelson. But there was a faint sense of relief in it, because it was not in any sense true that Nelson had murdered for her.

"Why is it impossible?" Crankshaw asked.

"Because he was over there, among the trees, when Stephen was killed. Nelson couldn't have been in that room and yet seen Mr. Luckett standing here with me, with his hand on my shoulder. He was over there, and he must have seen who came out of the house, but he's refused to admit that because he was glad my brother had been murdered."

She gestured towards the trees as she said it, and for an instant glanced towards them.

Among them something moved, a shadow among the shadows.

Crankshaw was shaking his head. There was a mild look of reproof on his face.

"That's what I thought," he said. "Your telling me that you and Mr. Luckett were sitting down here, when really you were standing up, that's what made all the difference. I came here and I sat down on the bench myself and tried to persuade myself Wingard could see round corners, because I always fancied him from the start, and more still once I picked up the scandal about him and Mrs. Luckett. But it wouldn't work. He couldn't have seen you from the window of the study if you'd been sitting down here, as you told me you were that first evening. But now stand up, Miss Gazeley, and look behind you."

Hilda stood up. She spun round. What she was expected to see she had no idea, and because all that she saw was entirely familiar, just as she had seen it, evening after evening, year after year, since she had come to live here with Stephen, the meaning of it totally escaped her.

Then Crankshaw stood up too and moved closer to her and put his hand on her shoulder. She saw this happen, not because she was looking at him, but because, with his rising from his uncomfortable seat on the heap of bricks, his shadow had suddenly lengthened out beside hers across the grass and mounted up the garden wall.

Printed there as clearly as in a cinema and easily recognisable, she saw her own head and Crankshaw's, and knew that anyone who had been at the window of Stephen's room, expecting to be able to escape through it, would have seen the shadows too. Also, she saw that anyone seeing only the two shadows, standing side by side with the man's hand on her shoulder, would have thought, as Nelson had thought, that they were embracing.

"Yes," she said, "I see."

Once more she glanced towards the trees. But that other shadow, tall, spare and stooping, had gone. There was nothing to be seen but oak and sycamore, birch and hazel.

She shivered again. Her coat no longer seemed to keep her warm.

"But you haven't really much proof yet, have you?" she said.

"Well, we've proof that it was Wingard, and not your brother, who obtained Lucy Cater's photograph. He's been identified by the man he dealt with. And it was Wingard who deliberately set to work to rouse your brother's interest in her. And your brother took the bait. Who wouldn't? She was a fascinating mystery, and for someone of your brother's tendencies—well, promising. But I think it was Wingard who telephoned her on Sunday morning, saying that he was your brother, and asking her to come here about the time he intended to commit the murder. She'd have made the perfect suspect for us, wouldn't she? He didn't reckon on Miss Perriman immediately packing her off out of the way and coming here herself instead, I suppose to try to buy your brother off, or to appeal to his better nature, but in any case, coming later than Mrs. Cater usually did, so that Wingard had got tired of waiting, gone in and killed your brother, and planted that photograph of Mrs. Cater on his desk."

"Yes, I see," Hilda said again.

She was thinking of Nelson, talking to her at lunch, trying to win her sympathy for the murderer, and also telling her the literal truth, that he had not seen anyone come out by the back door of the house and drop the hoe in the river.

But it had been a mistake to tell her of his lasting love for her. Intuition had served her, as it seemed it could not have served Valerie, to the point of telling her that

Nelson's loves would not be deep or lasting, and so, if only faintly, had stirred her suspicions.

But at least, knowing that he had been watching from the wood while she and Crankshaw were talking, and that he must have understood the meaning of what he had just seen, she had given him the chance, if he wanted to take it, to find a quicker way out of the dangers that faced him than the law would allow him.

It was probably the last chance that anyone would give him.

" And the fire? " she said.

" Oh yes, that was Wingard too," Crankshaw said. " He had two goes at it, the first time in the night after the murder. He'd got a heap of paper out of the desk on to the floor to start it and was ready to pour petrol around, when you came down and interrupted him. So he knocked you out, broke a window-pane to make it look as if an outsider had been searching the room, then tried again next day."

" But why? " she asked.

" Because he didn't want you, or anyone else, coming here in the evening, when shadows were long, to look at them as we've just been doing, and to start thinking about them."

She took a last look round, at the remains of the sunset, the ruins, and her shadow and Crankshaw's growing dim as the light faded. Then she turned to the gate.

" For that I'm grateful," she said.

Crankshaw walked at her side. As always there was a glint of cunning in his eyes, yet it seemed blended with the sympathy which he normally over-played so badly, but which now, in its moderation, was, for once, convincing.

" Where are you going now? " he asked. " To the Lucketts' house? They'll have a lot to bear, those young people, and Mr. Luckett too. Let me drive you over. You'll be needed there, Miss Gazeley."